TRACES

FINAL LAP

To Sue and Don

KINGFISHER

a Houghton Mifflin Company imprint

222 Berkeley Street

Boston, Massachusetts 02116

www.houghtonmifflinbooks.com

First published in 2007

2 4 6 8 10 9 7 5 3 1

LIBRARY OF CONGRESS CATALOGING-IN-PUBLICATION DATA
has been applied for.

ISBN-13: 978-0-7534-6005-4

Printed in India

1TR/0706/THOM/(MA)/90GSM/C

TRACES

FINAL
LAP

MALCOLM ROSE

KINGFISHER
BOSTON

Also available in the TRACES series:

Double Check
Framed!
Lost Bullet
Roll Call

Chapter One

Everything was wrong. It was the wrong time of year, and the sports stadium was not finished. The crowd was not really a crowd at all. A few trainers, athletes, reporters, and fans were bunched together in the only stand that had been completed so far. Seen from the airship overhead, they were a small oasis in a concrete desert, and the builders crawling busily over the rest of the arena looked like worker ants.

Only one competitor had reentered the stadium and embarked on the final lap. Approaching the end of the marathon, his gasps left a trail of steam behind him in the cold air. The weather was all wrong as well.

The giant telescreen at the far end of the stadium was blank. Once the electronics were fully installed, it would show pictures taken by the airship and outside cameras, trackside close-ups, and a list of the exact position of every runner in the marathon. For now, the leader's triumph was unannounced, but the large timer was showing *2:08:13.7*.

Jed Lester shook his head in disbelief. Without taking his eyes off the lead runner in the sky-blue uniform, he said to Owen Goode, "He's excellent, but the organizers are going to have to check the clock or the route. It's a practice run, out of season, and he's so young, yet he's coming in extremely close to the national record. They've probably messed up the distance."

Owen nodded. "Likely, it's short of the full forty kilometers."

The construction workers on the opposite stand stopped what they were doing and watched the lone runner completing a circuit of the track.

The event was a strange spectacle, designed to test Hounslow's preparations for hosting the International Youth Games in the spring. The volunteer runners were trying out the planned marathon route. The organizers were also checking the electronic timing system, the orientation of the airship, and a tagging device that monitored the position and order of every competitor throughout the long-distance event. After the finish line, they would also test the newly completed laboratory for detecting and measuring performance-enhancing drugs.

Jed had been a middle-distance runner. Twenty years ago, he was the best at more than 1,500 meters. Now, he'd teamed up with 15-year-old Owen Goode to develop a sports club in Greenwich. They were converting the old domed warehouse, built in a loop of the Thames river, into an indoor track and training facility. Already it was becoming a popular hangout for rebellious London kids who had run away from their schools. Jed was hoping to spot a new generation of athletes among them. He'd entered one boy and two girls into the trial marathon. Right now, he expected them to be 12 to 18 minutes away from the stadium.

Perplexed by the leader's performance, Jed stroked his trademark bald head with a cold hand and glanced down at the list that he'd been given. "Ford Drayton. On this showing, he'll be selected for the Games if the distance and time *are* right. But something must be wrong."

From across the track, there was a loud clunk and a metallic squeal. Thunderous hammering, pounding, shouting, and drilling had become commonplace during the construction of the stadium, so no one paid any attention. The noises were followed by a fearsome mechanical groan. Two builders, standing way up high on scaffolding, were resting their elbows on the steel railing and looking down at the closing stages of the race. From their lofty position, they could probably also see the other runners laboring along the outside walkway toward the stadium. Almost certainly, they would be able to see the full extent of Ford Drayton's lead over the following pack.

Watching Ford's tireless finish, Owen commented, "Maybe he's had a little help from drugs."

"I don't think so. It's not like it's a power event." Jed stared at Ford's wiry body as he came past the spectators' stand. "It's not his technique that's wrong, for sure," Jed said in admiration. "Look at his posture, how he holds his head. His arms pump beautifully, and his coordination's almost perfect, even after that distance. But if you're right and he *has* taken something, he'll be disgraced in an hour or two. That's LAPPED for you." Thinking of the Laboratory Analytical Procedure for Performance-Enhancing Drugs, Jed grunted. "In my day, lapped was something that happened to you on the track if you weren't very good. Back then, I had to race—and beat — the cheats. As simple as that."

Before Ford Drayton reached the finish line, there was an alarming creak from one section of the scaffolding. The sound was followed by a dreadful twang as the bolts holding up the platform on the left-hand side gave out. The planks of wood tilted and then tumbled down toward the track. The two builders who had been standing on them were tipped sideways as the planks slid out from under their feet. In a panic, they both grabbed the railing that they'd been leaning against. But the railing also came loose from the rest of the contraption, and the men were thrown into empty air.

Every face in the stand looked up—away from Ford's victory. Steel poles, three planks of wood, a girder, and two men plummeted to the ground. Yet their plunge seemed to last a lifetime. Their arms wheeled and legs flailed in slow motion.

A protracted human scream tore through the atmosphere. It was followed by the thud of wood hitting the trackside area and the clatter of a girder and steel railings. One of the metal shafts stabbed into the ground like an oversize javelin. But the worst was the silence that followed the dull thumps of the builders hitting the ground.

Focusing on his performance and maintaining his style in spite of exhaustion, Ford Drayton kept an eye on the stadium clock and paid no attention to the commotion behind him. He ran to the finish line in stunned silence. Only one spectator—his own trainer—applauded his remarkable achievement.

Forensic Investigator Luke Harding was listening carefully as the face on his telescreen described his next assignment. She was telling him about two construction workers who had lost their lives in the main sports stadium in Hounslow in the London area. Luke was puzzled, though. He asked, "Do you know for sure that it's suspicious? A scaffolding collapse sounds like an accident to me. Or bad work."

The representative of The Authorities seemed annoyed that Luke was questioning her word. She was probably aware that FI Harding had a growing reputation for dissent. But despite his youth, he also had a growing reputation for solving difficult cases. "It might sound like an accident to you, taken in isolation. But this isn't the first mishap at the Hounslow development. It began two years ago with an air traffic accident. I believe you know about it."

"Oh, yes," Luke replied. "I came across it in my last case. A Hounslow-to-Glasgow flight. Its fuel line wasn't right. Someone in maintenance attached the wrong nut. The pipe loosened during the flight, and fuel poured out."

"That's right. And one of the indoor sports venues went up in flames a few months ago. It had to be rebuilt. The first manager is missing, and there have been other incidents as well. I'll download details into your Mobile Aid to Law and Crime. We accept that accidents happen—but not this many. There comes a point when bad luck begins to look deliberate. We've reached that point. So, you'll investigate possible sabotage at the site."

"Have there been any deaths, aside from the passengers in the plane and these two builders?" he asked.

"Aren't they enough?" she responded. "We want you to catch the person or persons responsible before anyone else dies, and we want to know what happened to Libby Byrne. She was the site manager until she vanished. Her disappearance may or may not have anything to do with her work." The voice of The Authorities paused before adding, "There's a lot at stake here, Investigator Harding. Hounslow's a high-profile regeneration project. The biggest in the south of England by far. Despite the . . . difficulties, we're on the final lap, as far as construction's concerned. We don't want the International Youth Games jeopardized at this late stage. If this fails, it'll be our last attempt to renovate an area of London."

"That would be a pity." Luke was wondering if she was threatening to ax Owen Goode's alternative school in Greenwich as well.

"Make sure it doesn't happen, then."

"I'll do my best," Luke said toward her fading face.

When the principal of the Sheffield Music Collective appeared at Jade Vernon's door, Jade pulled her headphones down from her ears and let them rest on her shoulders, making a strange oversize necklace. She clicked the *Save* button to keep the samples that she'd added to a new mix of one of her pieces and swiveled toward him.

"Sorry to interrupt," he said, "but I have some news that you'll want to hear."

"Oh?"

"Good news," he stressed, beaming like a child. "It's from The Authorities, and I think you'll be pleased. Very pleased."

At once, Jade's thoughts turned to pairing. She was 16—four years from The Time—and she was hoping that The Authorities might have had a change of heart. Perhaps they would couple her with Luke Harding when The Time came. But would the Head of the Collective get involved in the business of the Sheffield Pairing Committee? Would he even know about her pairing situation and her wishes?

"Oh?" she repeated, wondering how long he was going to keep her in suspense.

"It's an honor for you and the whole Collective," he said. "The Authorities have commissioned you to compose the music for the opening ceremony of the International Youth Games and the official anthem." He clearly had more to say, but he hesitated in order to let the offer of the glitzy task sink in and to watch her reaction.

Her frown turned into a wide grin. "Really? The anthem? That's . . . brilliant. Amazing." In her excitement, she jumped to her feet and the headphone cable almost throttled her. "Fantastic. Why me, though?"

The principal replied, "Don't be so modest, Jade. It's obvious. You were selected because you're good. The best person for the job. Given the occasion, it's also appropriate for a youth—someone less than twenty—to provide the music."

Jade shook both of her fists in the air. "Yes! Fame at last."

"True. Previous writers of sports anthems have gone on to great things. I wish you well with it—as does everyone in the Collective."

"I can hardly believe it, but . . . I'll need a site visit," Jade said. "To get a feel for the place, to see what would work. Is that all right?"

"I assumed that you'd ask, so I've already checked. The main stadium is almost complete, so you can visit by arrangement almost any time. The other venues are at various stages of construction. Someone will take you wherever you want to go, as long as it's safe and doesn't interfere with the building."

"It's down near London, isn't it?" She tried not to pull a face.

The principal laughed. "Don't let that put you off. Think of yourself as part of the Hounslow regeneration scheme. It's a golden opportunity."

Despite the need to go to the South, she tingled all over. "I can't wait to get going," she said.

Chapter Two

It was very early in the morning. Brooke Adams was the only person in the huge swimming pool. She felt as if she was standing alone in a large, flooded cavern. The atmosphere was eerie and still. The windows at the far end of the pools and the lights overhead were perfectly reflected on the flat surface of the water. Brooke wasn't used to such calm. Whenever she stepped up to the edge of a pool, her supporters were normally chanting her name and encouraging her on to yet another win. Now, the spectators' gallery was empty. Her cough was the only sound, and it echoed back and forth across the empty space.

The Aquatic Center reeked. Brooke hadn't smelled anything like it before, but she imagined that it was normal for a brand-new facility.

She shook her arms and hands vigorously and wiggled her fingers. Then she moved her head from side to side and rotated her shoulders. Stretching the muscles of her sleek and supple body, she massaged the back of one leg and then the other. Keeping her legs straight, she bent down and touched her toes effortlessly. For a moment, she scratched them because they itched. Finally, she was ready. She was about to be the first person ever to enter this water.

She pulled her goggles down over her eyes and

perched at the side of the pool. Crouching into her starting position, she took a deep breath. Then she pulled her arms backward before throwing them forward and launching herself into the tranquil, unspoiled water.

She crashed through the mirrorlike surface, creating a chaos of ripples and a neat splash. Bubbles of air escaped from her nose as she executed one slow breaststroke underwater, before breaking the surface again. She propelled herself powerfully through the water, spearheading the wake behind her. Each sturdy stroke lifted her head and broad shoulders into the air. As the water fell back from her face, she sucked in a deep breath.

Around 30 meters down the length of the pool, though, she pulled up and, treading water, let out another cough followed by a pained cry. Her mouth, tongue, and throat seemed to be on fire. All of her exposed skin was burning as if it had been sandpapered. She stroked her stinging face with both hands. Her cheeks felt rough and ridged, like fingertips that had been in water long enough to go wrinkly. Convinced that there was something wrong with the pool, Brooke spat out the small amount of water that had gotten inside of her mouth and hurried to the side. As soon as her hands made contact with the edge, she yanked herself out. Feeling sick and screaming, she scampered to the poolside shower and dowsed herself with cold water.

* * *

Hounslow Residential was a large building riddled with long corridors and apartments, like a rabbit warren or an accommodation wing in a school. As with everything else in the area, it was not yet complete. The basic structure was in place but some of the living quarters, common rooms, and passageways had not yet been finished. There was a lot of bare plaster, wood, brick, and concrete on show. Everywhere there was the smell of paint and glue. The elevators seemed to have a mind of their own, stopping and starting at random, sometimes between floors. The water and electrical supplies were unpredictable.

The residence was run by two experienced managers and a lot of trainee staff. Aside from Luke and Malc, it seemed to be entirely occupied by builders. Many of them were temporarily living in Hounslow Residential while they worked on the regeneration project. Some were painters, putting the finishing touches on the plush accommodation block before it was used later in the year to house the best young athletes from around the world.

The variable quality and size of the meals suggested that the kitchen facilities were temperamental as well. The chefs were apprentices, and deliveries of food were as irregular as the elevators.

Seen from Luke's fourth-story window, Hounslow was awash with earth-moving vehicles and cranes. Scaffolding embraced many of the buildings like external skeletons.

A lot of hotels and restaurants were going up in time for the influx of athletes and spectators in the spring. Trees and shrubs had been cleared almost entirely from the site, but one large conifer towered beside Luke's room. To his right, the large Aquatic Center was complete but had not been officially opened. Workers were dismantling the steel framework and wooden planks that had surrounded it. Without taking his eyes off the industrial clutter, Luke said, "Anyone could wander around here in overalls and a hard hat, no questions asked. It'd be a perfect disguise. But who'd want to sabotage all this improvement or the Games themselves?"

Really, Luke was asking himself, but his computer answered, "You have not begun your investigation, so you do not have a list of suspects."

Luke shook his head. "No. I mean, what sort of person would want to throw a wrench in the works?"

"I have searched the case files and find no reference to a propelled tool causing damage," said the Mobile Aid to Law and Crime.

Luke smiled. His computer was a very clever and powerful piece of equipment but, in a way, stupid. "Open dictionary, Malc. A wrench in the works is a fly in the ointment." Knowing that his mobile would not let the matter rest, Luke stopped teasing him. "It means get in the way of, mess things up, sabotage. And I want to know who'd do it." He watched a team of workers crawling over the new medical center and physiotherapy unit, laying tiles on the roof. "Maybe the boss of a rival company that missed out on the building contract, or a construction worker who's been passed over for promotion. I don't know. How about an architect whose plans were turned down? And I guess the development might've stirred up grievances. I look at it and see all the good it's doing, but not everyone would, I suppose. Perhaps someone living here didn't want it at all. And there must've been other towns that thought they'd be chosen to host the Games, like somewhere up north that already has great facilities. Maybe someone there's determined to see Hounslow fail. Then there are athletes who haven't been selected for the Games."

"The Authorities had to evict several people from their homes to allow the scheme to proceed and, in particular, to lay the airport runway. They were offered superior accommodation. Most accepted alternative quarters, but some resisted and were removed by force. I have a file on them."

Luke nodded. "Yes, that's the type of thing. I want to build up a list of the sort of people who'd bear a grudge and might try to get revenge with a bit of sabotage."

"You have not yet proved that the series of accidents amounts to the crime of sabotage," Malc reminded him.

"Mmm. I don't suppose it's worth scanning building sites for evidence."

"Correct. There will be too much debris to distinguish significant traces. Also, you have not been called to the locations quickly enough. They will have been heavily contaminated, so any data would not be valid in law."

"Messiest crime scenes I've ever come across—if they are crime scenes." Luke dragged himself away from the window and lay down on the bed. "All right, let's review what's happened in the last two years. Talk me through it."

There was nothing in the sequence of incidents—from the loss of Flight GGW17 two years ago to the scaffolding collapse in the main stadium two days ago—that could definitely be put down to intentional interference. Each incident could have been the result of bad luck or bad work. Even the rifle that had blown up in the hands of one of the shooting team could have been a manufacturing fault. At least the shooter had survived the accident. The dump truck that went out of control might have had defective brakes from the start. There was no proof that the crash happened on purpose.

The mishaps had taken place across all of the Hounslow development. They weren't restricted to one part of the scheme or to one aspect of the International Youth Games. Sometimes builders had suffered, sometimes athletes, sometimes unconnected bystanders, like the passengers flying to Glasgow. But The Authorities were right. Luke found it hard to believe that so many things could go wrong with a project by mere chance.

One accident could be put down to bad luck; two were an unhappy coincidence; three or more had to be deliberate crime.

With his head on the pillow, Luke's feet overhung the end of the bed. "Tell me about Libby Byrne," he said to Malc.

"She is forty-two years old and trained in engineering. She was the Hounslow project manager until she failed to report for work three days ago. She left home in keeping with her normal schedule for the beginning of the week, but she did not arrive at her Hounslow office. There is no evidence for abduction or murder, but foul play must be suspected, given the number of related events."

"Anyone with a grudge against the development or the Games would have a grudge against her as well. I need to talk to her replacement and her partner."

"Logged."

"Do you have a register of everyone who worked in the aircraft maintenance center, when it was in operation?"

"Confirmed. However, it may not be complete."

"Did the accident inquiry find out which engineer attached the wrong nut on the fuel line?"

"No."

"Pity. He or she would've been my first suspect."

Malc said, "You should know that I have a list of spectators and competitors when the scaffolding collapsed in the main stadium. It includes Owen Goode and Jed Lester."

Luke got up on his elbows. "Really?"

"Correct. If they had not been present, I would not have told you the opposite."

Getting off the bed, Luke went for his coat. "Let's get going."

Malc hesitated and then announced, "I have received a transmission concerning the victim of an incident in the Aquatic Center yesterday. She is a swimmer named Brooke Adams. Doctors are suspicious about the cause and circumstances of the injuries. They believe it is a case of poisoning."

"Okay. Where is she?"

"Hounslow Medical Center."

"That's the first stop, then. But . . ." Luke glanced out of the window at the clinic. "It doesn't seem to have much of a roof yet."

Chapter Three

Brooke Adams was the thirteenth patient to be treated in the new center. Apart from the shooter whose rifle had exploded, all of the others had been builders who had been hurt in a variety of accidents, from the trivial to the serious. The medical center was far from finished and nowhere near fully staffed, so it was a relief that there were not many patients yet.

Brooke was sitting up in bed while, somewhere overhead, roofers hammered and drilled. Her appearance was upsetting. Aside from a small area around each eye, her face was rough and rippled like crumpled paper. The skin was more yellow, red, and blue than a healthy light brown. Her tongue was covered in sores, and she was itching all over. Bouts of vomiting and diarrhea had left her very weak. It was painful to see how an extremely healthy and pretty 18-year-old had been reduced to a shattered and disfigured wreck. But, the doctor had told Luke, at least she was now stable.

"They think there was poison in the water," she struggled to tell Luke. The ulcers on her tongue would not let her speak normally and clearly. The effort of forming words also seemed to exhaust her. "Do you know what it was? And why?"

Sitting next to her bed, Luke replied, "No, but I'll find out. The Aquatic Center's closed till I do. Did you see anyone around? Anything suspicious at all?"

She shook her head delicately. "The place was empty— weird, but nothing suspicious."

Her speech was badly slurred, and Luke had to concentrate in order to understand her. "I have to ask," he said. "Is there anyone who'd want to do this to you?"

"I don't think so. No." She lifted her knee and reached under the covers with her hand so that she could scratch the irritation between her toes.

"Did everyone know you'd be the first to go in the water? Was it announced?"

"No. I asked to try it before the formal opening."

Luke nodded. "In that case, if there was something in the pools, it would be aimed at anyone going in, not just you. It wasn't personal."

"That's worse, isn't it? A horrible idea." She took three deep breaths. A tube inserted into her nostril helped her get more oxygen. "I dread to think what would've happened without goggles. My eyes . . . you know."

"You can see all right?"

"Yes."

"That's good." Luke jerked his thumb toward Malc. "My mobile's downloaded all of your medical notes." He paused and asked him, "Haven't you?"

"Confirmed. The main symptoms are stomach pain,

23

fever, liver and kidney damage, jaundice, rapid heartbeat, lung damage, poor uptake of oxygen . . ."

"All right," said Luke, interrupting. When he looked at Brooke again, he wondered if she'd been told what the mystery substance had done to her face. He wondered if she had been given a mirror. He doubted it. He assumed that she'd have to deal with that shock later, when she had some of her strength back. Maybe the clinic was hoping that her complexion would improve before she saw it. "Is there anything else? The doctor doesn't want me here long. You have to rest."

"My . . . um . . ." She looked away in frustration and embarrassment.

"No problem. Take your time."

She gasped down more air. "My water's turned blue."

Before Luke could stop him, Malc said, "Please specify which water."

Luke put his hand on her arm. "Sorry. He's only a computer. He doesn't . . ." Turning toward Malc, Luke said quietly, "Her urine's blue. Does that help?"

"Confirmed," Malc replied. "The symptoms match those following exposure to paraquat."

"Paraquat?"

"It is a herbicide, used to kill broad-leaved weeds. It is toxic to humans by swallowing or by skin contact."

"Not exactly what you'd expect—or want—in a swimming pool." Affected by the plight of the likable girl,

Luke said to her, "I'll let you know when I find out more. You take care, all right?"

Brooke nodded softly.

Aside from his constant companion, Luke stood alone among the swimming pools. The water, tinged blue and yellow, looked calm and inviting. Perhaps, though, its appearance belied its true nature. Perhaps a secret lurked below the peaceful surface. "Take a sample, Malc, and analyze it for paraquat—or any other poison."

Malc drifted over the pool and then maneuvered himself until he was hovering a few inches above the water. Creating a ring of ripples, he used a narrow tube to suck up a small volume of the liquid and then returned to Luke. "Electrophoresis starting," he announced.

Luke crinkled his nose. "What's the smell?"

It took Malc three minutes to reply. "The fumes are nonhazardous solvents used in the construction, mixed with by-products of the disinfectant used in the pool."

"The air's safe, then?"

"Confirmed."

Without touching anything, Luke walked around the long pool and the diving area. There were three entrances to this part of the pools. One was from the men's changing rooms and another from the women's. The third was for staff and officials. There was also a poolside emergency exit that could be opened from the inside.

Access from the outside required the identity card of a member of staff, the emergency services, or a forensic investigator.

Malc announced the expected result. "The water is contaminated with a variety of toxic chemicals, the main component being paraquat. The highly toxic dioxin is also present. The mixture is too diluted to kill a human adult unless more than one liter is ingested, but it is sufficient to maim through skin contact."

Luke nodded. With the image of Brooke's crinkled and discolored face fresh in his mind, he added another trait to his list of possible saboteurs. He was looking for someone who was totally indifferent to the suffering of others. And he was now certain that he had a case of sabotage.

The number of accidents had already stretched his belief in coincidence. Now, the poisoning of Brooke Adams sent it far beyond breaking point because paraquat and dioxin could hardly have gotten into the water unintentionally. The polluting of the pool was an attack on Brooke and any other swimmer. It was the first clear instance of deliberate disruption, and in Luke's mind it raised the horrible prospect that the saboteur was stepping up the campaign against the Hounslow regeneration.

"This changes everything," he said. "No doubt about deliberate acts now. Try and find out when the pool was filled, Malc. That'll pin down the timescale for lacing the water."

"Searching."

"I know a thousand builders have been in and out, I know everything's covered in traces, but scan doorways anyway. Log everything in case we find the same thing at another site. That'd be helpful, to say the least."

"I cannot confirm that a thousand builders have entered the Aquatic Center. It may be fewer or more."

"Never mind," Luke muttered. "I'll tell you what we need now that we definitely have a crime. A codename for whoever's doing it. I'll call him or her Spoilsport. All right?"

"Codename entered."

"When you've finished here, we're going to Greenwich. I want to find out what Owen and Jed have to say."

Chapter Four

Luke took a cab to Isleworth and swiped his identity card through the quayside reader. Boarding a riverboat, he asked for North Greenwich. A cruiser on the Thames river was a surer and safer option than an electric cab into central London. Cabs were more likely to be ambushed by bandits, and a lot of freeways and corridors were blocked by trees and shrubs that had broken through the asphalt. In some places, the power had been cut by out-of-control wildlife or collapsed buildings, and some bridges had fallen down.

Luke stood at the prow of the cruiser as the onboard computer navigated the winding turns of the Thames river. He was looking forward to seeing Owen and Jed again, but he felt sad as he watched a succession of rundown and flood-damaged areas of London slip past.

At his side, Malc reported, "According to data on the site manager's computer, the Hounslow swimming pool was filled with water fifteen days ago."

Luke groaned. "So it could have been poisoned for a couple of weeks. If that's right, there's no hope of getting any clean evidence." He shook his head and brushed some stray hairs away from his face. "Check with herbicide suppliers for any unusual orders of paraquat. Or theft."

"Searching."

When the riverboat surged under Westminster Bridge, Luke felt like ducking down and covering his head with his hands—just in case. The structure was on its last legs, but something solid was stopping it from tumbling into the Thames river.

A few more twists and turns, and the cruiser powered down as it passed the huge battered warehouse. The boat glided up to the jetty and engaged automatically with the attachments. Wasting no time, Luke jumped ashore and headed toward the sports club.

As soon as the kids saw him, they recognized him as an FI because of his Mobile Aid to Law and Crime. Several of them ran away. They didn't want to be questioned about how they came to be at the converted dome. Really, it was habit that made them shy of investigators. Luke posed no threat to them because he'd made sure that The Authorities approved of the Greenwich club. It was no longer against the law to skip school and meet there for training.

"Hi," Luke said to Owen with a smile.

Owen put his hands on his hips and sighed heavily. "You're still frightening kids."

Luke could tell from Owen's face that he wasn't really annoyed. "My specialty. Sorry."

"You won't catch them. Jed's got them trained up to be champions."

In Owen and Jed's unlikely partnership, Owen provided youthful enthusiasm and Jed provided the expertise. Both had credibility with the kids, but, importantly, Jed had credibility with The Authorities because he was a sports hero. His 1,500 meters record set at York Races still stood.

The two boys walked farther into the monstrous dome. "Whenever we get together," Luke said, "there's always a disaster lurking somewhere. It started with a lost bullet in your shoe . . ."

Owen interrupted with a grin. "Wasn't lost to me. It was in my heel. Still got the hole to prove it. Wasn't much of a disaster, either. I didn't get killed, and you got the bad guy who fired it. With my help."

"You also persuaded me to double-check Everton Kohter's death sentence."

"You cracked that. No disaster, with my help again. And I got you a clue in your Emily Wonder case."

"So, how are you going to help me catch whoever's trying to ruin the International Youth Games?"

Owen shrugged. "Didn't know I was going to."

Jed joined them, asking, "Is that what it is? Someone trying to bring the Games down?" He was clearly appalled.

"Yes."

With a grin, Owen said, "Some of our kids would love to see the Hounslow stadium come crashing down." Realizing that the other two were much more serious, he added, "Not really. Just . . . dreaming."

"Why?" Luke asked.

"Because they think that then the Games would have to move here."

Jed shook his head. "And that's why it's fantasy. Silly talk. The roof leaks, no seating for spectators, no decent transportation, hopeless lighting, and don't get me started on the state of the changing rooms. We haven't even gotten rid of all the sludge from the tsunami flood or replaced the panels that it ripped away. Let's get real. The Hounslow Games have got to go ahead," he said. "You must not let anything stand in their way. They're the most important thing. They're a sign of hope, that someone cares. Something for youngsters to aim for. I wish I was their age again. I'd love to be part of it, competing against the best."

At the far end, a noisy game of baseball was underway. Several young people were jogging around the newly laid indoor track. A few sprinters were practicing their starts along one side, and a lanky boy threw himself up and arched impressively over the high-jump bar. Two girls were playing darts on the right. There were archery targets as well, but no one was using them at the moment. They reminded Luke of competitions at his school. He had a knack for almost any sport that required careful aim, and he used to beat everyone at archery.

He said, "You were both in the stadium when the scaffolding came down. What did you see?"

"Nothing," Owen answered. "Just . . . you know. Two blokes falling." Grimacing, he added, "Not nice."

"Was there anyone else up near them? Someone who didn't fall?"

"We weren't watching the builders," Jed explained. "A lad was finishing the marathon. Ford Drayton. That's what we had our eyes on. Like everyone else. He came in close to the national record. There was an inquiry after the race, but the clock and route were correct. He'll be in the Games now. Something strange is going on there. If you ask me, you should investigate Ford Drayton as well as the accident."

"Nothing showed up on LAPPED, either," Owen added. "So it's not drugs."

Trying to stick to the point, Luke said, "When the platform gave out, you must've looked up. What did you see?"

"The airship," Owen answered. "And the bits and pieces coming down."

"An airship," Luke muttered. "Interesting." He gazed at Jed, prompting another answer.

Jed shrugged. "Sorry. Nothing."

It was Luke's turn to sigh. Trying not to show his disappointment, he said, "Never mind. Do you have anyone good enough for the Games?"

"A couple for certain," Jed replied. "A couple more, maybe." He paused before continuing, "If you're on a case, you ought to get in shape and enter an event. To get an insider's view."

Luke laughed. "I'm nowhere near Games standard in anything."

Jed said, "I can get you up there in the eight hundred meters, if you've got the determination."

"Yeah? And how long would that take?"

"Not by tomorrow, that's for sure. Weeks and months."

Luke shook his head. "Thanks, but . . . it's not going to happen. Unfortunately. Besides," he added, pointing at the top of Jed's shorn head, "I can't see myself with the runner's hairstyle."

On the way back to Hounslow, Luke complained, "That was a wild-goose chase."

Malc said, "Incorrect."

Luke turned toward him. "Why? What did you spot that I didn't?"

Apparently confused, the mobile hesitated before responding, "It is incorrect that a game bird was your objective."

Luke waved his hand dismissively. "Here we go again! A wild-goose chase means a waste of time. Put it in your dictionary. I suppose I got one thing out of it. The airship, Malc. Check if it was taking pictures of the stadium. If it

33

was, get copies."

"Logged."

"Do you have anything on sources of paraquat?"

"Yes."

"Tell me, then."

"After the airplane crash destroyed Coventry Chemical Industrial Zone two years ago, a new manufacturing zone was set up to the west of the Midlands. This is the unit that now provides most paraquat and other herbicides and pesticides. Farms are by far the major users. The chemical industry has not noted unusual consumption or excessive orders. However, a new customer has been the Hounslow scheme. A large quantity of herbicide was required to combat an infestation of weeds and other flora before and during regeneration."

The chilly wind that was blowing into Luke's face made his nose run. He wiped it and said, "I bet no one would notice a few barrels missing from the building site. Looking anywhere else for it would probably be another wild-goose chase."

Chapter Five

The manager's office was a large temporary trailer positioned in front of a series of huge wind turbines that provided a lot of the power for the regeneration scheme. The roomy headquarters had windows on three sides, providing a view over most of the development, dominated by the impressive arch over the main stadium. To receive all of the incoming messages, the telescreen was permanently turned on. There were four sets of overalls and hard hats hanging on one wall, three pairs of reinforced shoes below, and a state-of-the-art computer terminal on the central desk.

Telling Luke about his new role, Neil Gladwin seemed to be reciting a speech. "It's not about me. The main point of all of this," he said, sweeping his hand widely, "is the legacy that we leave behind. Young people in London shouldn't have to go to crumbling sports clubs with miserable facilities. This venue and the Games will be stepping-stones to participation in sports, transforming young lives, inspiring tomorrow's athletes, and providing community focus. My goal is rejuvenating Hounslow and providing a resource that'll benefit all of London for generations to come. I know there've been teething problems, but we're focused now. I'm determined that

we'll meet whatever challenges remain and strengthen our investment in the development because the purpose is worth it." He might have rehearsed the words, but he sounded sincere.

Luke nodded. "I guess Libby Byrne had the same attitude."

"More or less."

"You were her deputy until she disappeared. How did you two get along?"

Neil shrugged. "The usual creative tensions, that's all."

"Not very well, you mean."

"In sports, different coaches train their athletes in different ways. It's the same in engineering. Libby had her way of managing a big project, and I have mine. I'll bring it in on time with the quality that everyone expects."

"What exactly was she working on when she disappeared?" Luke asked.

"In this game, you've got a lot of balls in the air at the same time, but . . ." Neil stood up and pointed out of one of the windows. "See the big pillars over there? New this week. They'll be the front of the indoor arena for tennis, squash, gymnastics, darts, and a few other things. The back of it will be the tee-off point for golf."

"Yes?"

"On my first day in charge, I inherited an issue about the type of concrete to be used. That's what she was trying to deal with on the evening before she disappeared. I've taken care of it."

Luke said, "Was she in any sort of trouble?"

"Not that I know of."

"Where were you on the morning that she failed to show up?"

"Me?" He looked astonished that Luke would ask.

"Nothing to worry about," Luke replied. "If she's been abducted, I want to know where someone snatched her. I can rule out wherever you were—because you would've reported it."

"I was here at work, as always." Neil looked away and then let out a weary breath. "To be honest, she treated me like you treat that," he said, pointing at Malc. "A machine. Get this done, do that. And she was never shy about taking the credit when I got things moving ahead of schedule."

Luke was tempted to think that there was a parallel between himself and Libby. He wanted to keep his mind on the interview, but for a second he wondered whether he was always fair to his mobile. Did he take the credit for completing a case when much of his success was down to Malc's activities? But there was a big difference between his relationship with Malc and Libby's with Neil. Malc *was* a machine. Credit meant nothing to him. "Do you have a record of where every drum of paraquat went?"

Neil was taken aback. "Er . . ." He glanced at his

computer. "No. We don't keep that sort of detail, or we'd drown in data. Why?"

"Never mind."

A security alert appeared on the manager's telescreen. The head and shoulders of a member of the airport staff explained, "Old Frank Russell's at it again, Neil."

Neil glanced at Luke and said, "Excuse me." He turned toward the telescreen and asked, "What's he done now?"

"He's sitting in the middle of the airstrip."

"What? When's the next flight due?"

"Not for an hour-and-a-half. But . . ."

Luke interrupted. "Is this some sort of protest against the regeneration?"

Neil nodded. "Not his first, either. I'll send security guards in to move . . ."

"No," Luke replied. "I'll go and talk to him. It's not like there's a plane waiting to land or take off."

Neil shrugged. "Feel free. I'm not going to grumble if you take a job off my hands." He said toward the telescreen, "There's an FI coming over. Name of Luke Harding. He'll sort it out."

Luke walked out of the airport terminal carrying a chair in each hand. When he reached the middle of the runway, he looked down at Frank Russell lying uncomfortably on the concrete and said, "Brought you a seat." He put it down by the old man. He positioned the other across from the first and sat down himself. "It's cold out here," he added with a shiver. "Nothing to stop the wind. And it'll be dark soon."

Frank eyed him suspiciously. "What's your game?"

"They're getting a load of security guards together in there," he said, jerking his thumb toward the terminal. "They'll come and move you soon. So, you have a choice. Wait for the big thugs or talk to me."

"Who are you?" He struggled to lean on his elbows, but the aches and pains of old age stopped him. Recognizing a Mobile Aid to Law and Crime beside Luke, he said, "Are you old enough to be an investigator?"

Malc replied, "Forensic Investigator Harding graduated from Birmingham School with an unprecedented set of marks. At sixteen years of age, he is lacking in experience, but his success rate is one hundred percent."

"My name's Luke," he said to Frank. "Have a seat." He waved toward the other chair.

"All right." Frank groaned as he got to his feet and then lowered himself into the chair.

Luke looked around and grinned. "You know, I've never sat in the middle of a runway before. We must look pretty silly. And don't you feel nervous, even if the next flight's not due for a while?"

"It's worth it," Frank replied.

"Why's that?"

Frank sighed. "You've seen the development. It's

spreading across Hounslow like a cancer. Turned it into a no-man's-land. It was my place. A bit rundown, I grant you. Maybe more than a bit. It had its problems. But it was a good home for me and a few others. It had character. Not now. Over there," he said, pointing, "just on this side of the control tower, I had a greenhouse. Grapes and peaches, I grew. From there to here were gardens. My own garden. Lovely, juicy plums and strawberries. Almost an orchard. Potatoes, cabbage, spring onions, crispy lettuce. You won't grow anything here now. And pigeons. I had a loft, and I bred them, the birds. I could recognize every one. Even blindfolded, I could do it just by cupping them in my hands." He hung his head and shook it sadly. When he looked up again, he said, "See the what-do-you-call-it . . . the maintenance center? They closed it down because an engineer couldn't put a nut on a pipe properly and brought a plane down. Anyway, one of my neighbors built his own reptile house there. Rickety maybe, but . . . all ruined. All gone. For what? An airstrip that's hardly used, cab corridors, a concrete terminal, those monsters waving their arms in the wind. What a waste. You should've seen my pigeons. Rare breeds, some of them. Lovely blue-plumed birds." He turned to Luke and added, "But no one around here listens."

"I'm listening."

"But it's too late, and you're not The Authorities. How

could they treat us like that?"

Luke didn't want to be drawn into speaking for The Authorities, but he replied, "Didn't they offer you a nice apartment?"

Frank shook his head and grimaced. "Not the same. My neighbor resisted for a while before he took a place in Ealing, but I can't walk away. I get so angry when I see Hounslow now. He doesn't. He's too old. He doesn't remember how it used to be. The airport wiped out his little nest, and his memories went with it. It's the shock that made him go downhill."

"But, you said yourself, it's too late. I don't know what we're doing, sitting out here, waiting for a plane to mow us down."

"I've got to get my protest in. I've got to have my say before . . . This is one way of doing it. I know it doesn't do any good, but . . ."

It was obvious that the old man was desperate and angry. Luke doubted that he was angry enough to be Spoilsport, though, because he also seemed helpless. "This isn't your first bit of direct action, is it?"

Frank shook his head. A faint smile came to his lips as he brought his exploits to mind. "I've sat in all sorts of places. In front of bulldozers, on foundations and piles of bricks to stop them from building, on cab tracks to stop workers from arriving, on cranes. Everywhere. I've become an expert at sitting in uncomfortable places."

Luke laughed and then looked to the right, where Malc hovered. "You told me that you had a file on objectors who'd been evicted. Is Frank Russell in it?"

"Yes."

The old man chuckled to himself.

Luke returned the smile. "You're famous. I'll hear all about you later. Have you ever gone in for loosening nuts and bolts?"

Frank wiped the amusement from his face. "I wish I had the guts. But it'd be dangerous. Mine's a peaceful campaign."

"Is there anyone else who'd go further than you?"

"I don't think so."

"It's going to be nice around here when they've finished it. That's how I see it. And after the Games, when it's all died down, maybe there'll be a little corner for you. With your own garden."

"Huh. Won't be the same. I'll be gone by then, anyway."

"Gone where?" asked Luke.

Clearly wondering how to answer, Frank watched two large rats scampering across the airstrip and disappearing into the grass at the edge. "This building site isn't the only cancer." He placed his fist against his chest. "Lungs don't last forever."

"I'm sorry," Luke said.

"What are you going to do with me now?"

Luke shrugged. "Plenty of options. Make the plane

circle till you give up, fall asleep, or keel over through lack of food, or wait till the cold gets you. But the manager or The Authorities will probably send the guards in before that, and you'll be moved by force. They might order me to arrest you on a charge of obstruction and question you about sabotage. It could get heavy and unpleasant." Luke stood up and grabbed the back of his chair. "Or you could walk away with me before it gets ugly. You've made your point."

Frank sniffed. "You're all right for an FI. Better than the guards who usually carry me off. Most undignified for someone my age."

Luke smiled at him again. "Come on. Let's go and get warm."

"I suppose so," Frank replied.

Luke carried the chairs away. Glancing at Frank as he made his way to the terminal, Luke couldn't easily envisage him climbing high up on scaffolding in the main stadium and interfering with bolts. His walk was more of a shuffle. He barely raised his feet, so his shoes scraped noisily along the ground. Unless he was exaggerating his infirmity, it was difficult to imagine him abducting or murdering a healthy Libby Byrne. Even so, Frank was clearly determined to make his protest, despite his age and frailty. Luke asked, "When you had this garden, did you use paraquat?"

He looked puzzled. "What's that?"

"A herbicide."

Frank pulled a face. "I believe in these," he said, holding up his withered hands. "Hard work, not chemicals, for getting rid of weeds."

Chapter Six

Walking toward Hounslow Residential, taking a detour around a half-built factory that would soon make and repair sports equipment, Luke said, "At least I've got my first two suspects, even if they're not exactly convincing."

As always, Malc needed precision. "Please specify names."

"I'm talking about Frank Russell and Neil Gladwin."

"There is no evidence against Neil Gladwin."

"No," Luke admitted. "But before he was promoted, he had a motive. He was feeling angry about being the deputy and not the boss. He had plenty of opportunities—and the know-how—to make sure that things went wrong for Libby Byrne. And he's done well out of her disappearance. He got the top job."

"Two acts of sabotage have occurred since he took over as project leader: the collapse of scaffolding in the main stadium and the swimming pool poisoning."

"He could've messed with the scaffolding and doctored the water in the pool two weeks ago, while Libby was still in charge," Luke replied. "Maybe he got impatient in the meantime and killed her instead. Afterward, he couldn't drain the pool secretly. And going up the scaffolding to undo whatever he'd done would've

45

been too risky, too awkward to explain if he was spotted. Anyway, if all the sabotage stopped as soon as he took over, it'd be a bit obvious, wouldn't it? He might want it to carry on for a bit so that he doesn't look guilty."

"That is valid reasoning."

Luke continued, "I'm not so sure about Frank Russell, though, even if he is in your file of troublemakers. High on motivation, low on capability, I figure. And it's hard to believe that a man who lies down on a runway will poison a swimming pool, crash an airplane, or do away with a manager. It's in a different league." He hesitated before adding, "I suppose, if he's as ill as he claims, he doesn't have anything to lose. But he doesn't have anything to gain, either. Just revenge before he dies. He didn't work in aircraft maintenance a couple of years ago, did he?"

"He is not in my database of service engineers."

"Check his medical records. See if he really is ill."

"Searching."

"I still don't think he's Spoilsport. He's frightened by change, that's all. Like a lot of people, especially old ones. It doesn't make him dangerous, just scared."

Even though his apartment was on the top floor, Luke opted out of using the elevator. He charged up the stairs two at a time. On the third level of the apartment block, the supervisor was busily directing a whole gang of trainee staff and decorators to rearrange one of the rooms. On his way past, Luke lingered to look inside. The living quarters were bigger and better than his own.

The manager greeted him and then said excitedly, "We're being visited by the Games' official musician tomorrow. Our top suite's been reserved for her."

Luke grunted. "She's being treated better than an FI."

"The composer's always a very special person."

"And an investigator isn't." He smiled to show that he wasn't serious. "Actually, I know a fantastic musician who'd do a terrific job. The trouble is, no one would be able to drag her south of Birmingham." He walked toward his own room.

Needing a drink, Luke turned on the cold water faucet. For a second, nothing happened. Then the pipe let out a violent clunk, and water came out in a sudden violent spurt. It was light brown, like the color of skin. Hitting the sink, the gush of water splashed everywhere, soaking Luke's sweater and pants. He stepped back and muttered a curse. Then he said, "I bet that doesn't happen in the official musician's room. I bet everything's perfect in there." Shaking his head, he went for a towel.

Later, he sat in front of the telescreen and looked at Jade's playful face. "You're looking pleased with yourself. What's going on?"

She shrugged. "Just had a good day, that's all. I'll play you a new piece sometime."

In a way, the telescreen narrowed the distance between them. In a way, it also emphasized their

separation. Luke looked at her and said, "You've gone blonde."

Jade ran a hand through her hair. It looked as if she'd already disturbed it about a hundred times, or she'd been outside in a gale. "Good, isn't it?"

"Always," said Luke. "Hey. I might meet someone you know tomorrow."

"Oh? Who's that?"

"I don't know her name, but I bet you do. She's doing the music for the International Youth Games. She's staying here, apparently."

"Lucky her."

"To be staying with me, you mean?"

Jade laughed. "No. I mean, whoever got that job is on to a winner. Fame's just around the corner."

"If you want, I could murder her and then you might get it instead."

"I wouldn't do that, if I were you. Malc did his best to arrest you when you got framed at school. He'd definitely get you for doing in a high-profile musician. Anyway, I wouldn't want the job as a substitute. I'd be annoyed that I wasn't the first choice."

At once, Luke looked away from the larger-than-life version of Jade.

"What have I said?" she asked.

"Sorry. You just made me think of a substitute building manager I met today. He has the job he wanted, but he might still be angry because he wasn't the first choice. Thanks. Interesting idea."

"Glad to be of service," Jade replied.

"Yeah. I'll tell you who the Games' musician is and what she's like, if I bump into her. But she won't be up to your standard."

Jade smiled at him. "You never know. She might be just as brilliant as me."

Her image faded away, and, once again, Luke was left with a sophisticated metal box for company.

Malc projected a movie of the closing stages of the marathon onto the telescreen. The aerial images had been shot from the airship. When the movie zoomed in on Ford Drayton, Luke lost interest. It was the wide shots of the incomplete stadium that captured his attention.

Several times, he asked Malc to pause the video and home in on the scaffolding. He was able to watch the two builders take a break, lean on the railing, and peer down at the track. Horrifyingly, Luke could watch the contraption give out and tip the men over. The movie followed their long, dreadful descent, their arms and legs thrashing uselessly in the air. Luke was appalled but no wiser. There was no one else near them when they fell. Luke was disappointed that he couldn't get an image of Spoilsport, but the movie fit in with his theory that the bolts had been sabotaged some time before the coming

and going of the builders worked them completely loose.

It was getting late when Luke finally admitted defeat and gave up examining the overhead pictures.

A Mobile Aid to Law and Crime never tired, though. Malc told him, "Frank Russell's medical records do not contain any reference to serious illness."

The result jolted Luke because it was not what he expected. "What? He doesn't have cancer?"

"Correct."

"So why did he tell me he did?" Luke wondered.

"Unknown," Malc replied. "However, I am programmed to assume that suspects may not tell the truth."

"Yeah," Luke said. "He might be lying because he's Spoilsport, pretending that he's not well enough to go up scaffolding and the like." Luke thought about it for a few seconds. "There's another reason you wouldn't understand. It has to do with human nature. He's feeling sorry for himself. Maybe he invented the cancer as a way of getting sympathy. The Authorities haven't just evicted an old man; they've evicted a dying man. Sounds a lot worse. He might even have convinced himself that he's ill."

"According to the file on objectors, he has a long record of interfering with the regeneration . . ."

Luke interrupted. "He didn't deny it. He's more into making himself a nuisance than turning nasty."

"Frank Russell's known opposition to the Hounslow

project and the pretense regarding his fitness make him the prime suspect," Malc stated.

"All right," Luke replied. "Next time security guards haul him away from his latest protest, get them to bring him to me."

"Task logged."

Chapter Seven

The next morning, Malc guided Luke to the Experimental Technology Institute, where Libby Byrne's partner was a researcher. Like Libby, Royston Klein was an engineer, but he was using his training in an entirely different field. He was working on the production of high-tech clothing.

Luke held out his identity card and said, "I'm here about Libby."

Immediately, Royston stopped fiddling inside of a yellow Lycra vest and gazed at him. "Have you found her?" he asked.

"Sorry. No. I want to ask you a few questions to help me find her."

"Ah."

He seemed relieved. Luke wasn't sure of the reason. Perhaps Royston lived in fear of an announcement that her body had been discovered. Or perhaps he didn't want her to turn up at all. To provoke him, Luke remarked, "You don't seem very worried."

"With all due respect, you don't know what I'm feeling. Libby and I did our duty twenty years ago. We were paired. We had two children. We delivered them to school, then we got on with our lives . . ."

"Separately?"

"We live together but more or less independently. Don't get me wrong, though." He stroked his beard, about four days' worth of stubbly growth. "We're good companions. We have a lot of respect for each other."

To Luke, he seemed like another victim of the pairing process, another partner who'd settled for respect instead of love. On Luke's left, a computer monitor showed a line shooting repetitively across the screen. Around once a second, it formed a fleeting peak in the middle of the display, and the system let out a short, high-pitched tone at the same time.

"Go back four days," Luke said. "The beginning of the week. She left home at what time?"

"Seven-thirty. Almost exactly. As always."

"Did she seem all right?"

Royston shrugged. "I think so."

"Did she take a cab?"

"As far as I know, yes."

"Did you go out after her?"

Royston glared at him for an instant. "What's that supposed to mean? Am I a suspect?"

"Anyone who has something to do with her is a suspect until I prove that they're not. You may well have been the last person to see her, so I'm bound to be interested in you."

"I left for work around seven-forty-five. Fifteen minutes after she left. And no, I didn't see her outside."

"Have you heard from her since?"

"No."

"What was she wearing?"

Royston thought about it for a moment. "I didn't notice, but she would've had a full-length leather coat on—because she always did."

"Was she carrying anything?"

"She had a brown briefcase. I guess she took that. Probably nothing else."

"Did she have a pairing ring on?"

"Yes. And a watch. That's it, though."

Distracted by the bleeping computer, Luke nodded toward it. "What is that? Sounds like something in a hospital."

Royston smiled and nodded. "Exactly. It's my heartbeat."

Luke was surprised. "How does it know what your heart's doing?"

Royston undid the top two buttons of his shirt to reveal a tight-fitting yellow garment. "It's called haptic clothing. "Haptic" means based on the sense of touch. You see," he said, buttoning up his shirt and pointing to the same sort of Lycra garment attached to a dummy, "it has wireless sensors all over the inside, touching the body underneath. The one I've got on is monitoring my heart from chest vibrations. Don't they say someone's heart rate goes up if they tell a lie?" He shrugged. "Now that I'm a suspect, you can tell if I wander from the truth just by listening to my heartbeat."

"The method is not sufficiently reliable," Malc said.

"Some people sweat when they lie," Luke added.

"It'd be easy to design a haptic garment that measures the electrical conductance of skin. That'd change when sweat's around."

Intrigued, Luke asked, "What are you using it for?"

"I can think of lots of applications, but I'm looking at health," Royston answered. "These clothes could track quite a few body functions. Imagine that I had a heart condition. The feedback from my haptic vest would give me—and a clinic—the earliest possible warning of a problematic rhythm. It could be a lifesaver."

Luke noted that Royston seemed more animated about his research than about the disappearance of his partner. But his face and manner were hard to read.

Against a background of the regular bleeps, Luke returned to the subject of the Hounslow development. "How was Libby doing at work? She must've said something."

"It was a lot of responsibility. If she was here, she'd probably admit that she was struggling with the workload. But she wasn't helped by some guy named Neil. Always undermining her, she said."

"She had a lot of bad luck to deal with as well."

Royston grunted. "Huh. She didn't believe in luck. She thought that someone was trying to ruin the whole show."

"Did she have a feeling for who that might be?"

This time, Royston's smile was twisted. "I think I just told you."

"Neil Gladwin?"

"That's the one."

"Did she have any evidence?"

"Yes. Her intuition. And a work colleague who was clearly after her job."

"I don't think that her feelings are going to convince Malc," Luke replied wryly.

Royston ignored his remark.

"Was there any reason that she might leave of her own accord?"

"No," Royston answered quickly.

"Maybe work was getting her down . . ."

"Not that much," said Royston. "I may look cool about Libby, you know, but inside I'm . . ." He thumped his chest, and his heartbeat monitor went into convulsions. The computer screen filled with crazy peaks and troughs, and the bleeping went wild. "Oops. Shows you it works." He composed himself before adding, "She doesn't deserve . . . Anyway, I want her back. Alive and unharmed."

Luke nodded. "I'm working on it." He turned to go but pretended to change his mind. Making sure that his face remained deceptively expressionless, he said, "I'm curious. What do you think of the Hounslow scheme. Do you approve?"

Royston hesitated and exhaled noisily. "It can't be a bad thing. Good for kids."

"Yeah," Luke replied. "That's right." But he wasn't sure why Royston's heart rate had increased slightly.

Back in Hounslow, Luke stood in wonderment at the huge stadium with its track surrounded by layer upon layer of seating and, above it all, a giant arch. It was much more impressive in reality than in the overhead clips from the airship. Right now, the temporary supports, dumpsters, cranes, and containers made it a mess, of course, but it was going to be magnificent. Luke had been in London long enough to realize that he was inside of something extraordinary. The sports stadium was a heartbeat that meant the city might not be dying after all. Luke could not allow a rogue saboteur to wreck London's fragile revival. Leaning on the trackside railing, he could also understand Jed's passion for bringing the Games and young athletes to this venue.

In the temporary steel network across from him, interlocking ladders led up to platforms slung under the canopy, high above Luke. The builders working up there seemed to form a separate tier of life. Most people went about their normal lives with their feet firmly on the ground. The sky was the habitat of birds and aircraft. In between, the Hounslow construction workers were bustling around on scaffolding.

Luke's eyes followed the zigzag flights of steps from the ground to the upper tier, and he let out a whistle. "That's a lot of ladders to climb. I wonder if Frank Russell's up to it."

"Insufficient data," Malc answered.

"Mmm." Luke's head felt unusually heavy and unbalanced because of the hard hat that he was required to wear while he was in the stadium. "I'm going to take a look at the parts that took the quick way down. Come on."

He vaulted over the barrier and set off across the area for the track and field events. In a few months' time, there would be expert runners pounding the track. Anyone crossing the middle then would be in extreme danger from javelins, discuses, or hammers. Outside of both straights, various jumping events would be taking place. The crowd might be applauding a run up to the long jump. Right now, the only sounds were hammering, drilling, and builders shouting to each other. There were no athletes on show at all. On the far side, Luke stooped to examine the fallen fragments of scaffolding that had been collected and stacked beside the track.

"They have been moved and contaminated," said Malc. "No legal evidence can be collected from them and entered into case files."

Luke was inspecting the end of a girder. "There's a hole

through here," he said. "I guess that's where a bolt went."

"Correct."

"No marks or anything." He shrugged. Looking around at the ground, he spotted a pile of 12 large nuts and bolts, but he didn't touch them. "Well, the bolts didn't snap. It wasn't metal fatigue. Either they weren't twisted tight enough in the first place, or Spoilsport took the nuts off, dropped them overboard, and left vibrations to shake the bolts out. A careless worker might leave one nut loose by accident, but not all twelve. That's more than careless. So I figure that this is Spoilsport's work." He looked up at Malc. "I know that they wouldn't be valid, but are there any prints on these nuts and bolts?"

"There are many partial and overlapping fingerprints. The patterns are too complex and incomplete to analyze."

"Anything else? Like hair or fibers?"

"There are fibers typical of all builders' overalls. I do not detect hair, skin, or other human traces."

"Pity." Luke stood up and stretched himself like an athlete about to run a race. Looking regretfully down the home straight, he said, "This is the closest I'll get to running in any games. A shame. I would've . . . Anyway, I've got a crime to solve."

Leaving his hard hat in the bare reception room, Luke asked Malc, "Are there any parts around here that are actually finished?"

"According to the plans downloaded in my memory, a practice gymnasium and two training grounds are complete and available to sports teams."

"A gym. Take me there." Outside again, Luke waved his hand in the direction of the indoor arena with its ornate pillars. "All this reminds me of how much I enjoyed sports at school. I was pretty good, you know. I should get in shape."

"You have a perfectly adequate shape," Malc responded.

Luke spread his arms as he walked. "Well, thanks for the compliment."

"I calculate that your calorific input equals your energy requirements on average. Therefore, you are not increasing or decreasing your mass. Also, the results from the automatic sampler in the last smart toilet that you used indicate good health."

Luke laughed. "I didn't know you cared so much about me."

"I am programmed to protect you in all possible ways. You are a valuable asset to The Authorities."

"Ah. That's it, is it? I'm an asset."

"Confirmed," Malc replied.

Luke knew it all along, really. The Authorities had invested a lot in his training as a forensic investigator. They wanted to protect that investment. Malc was not really a friend. He was an unsentimental tool designed to keep Luke safe, to perform forensic procedures, and to make sure that FI Harding followed the requirements of the law. But, to Luke, Malc felt more like a friend than a mere companion.

Luke swiped his identity card through the reader, entered the gym, and headed toward the visitors' gallery. There, he looked down on ten young people, all wearing their team's sleek, sky-blue uniforms. Three were running powerfully on machines yet remaining stationary. A couple were lifting weights. Two more were heaving energetically on rowing machines. One was performing regular exercises on mats and bars. In the middle, the team leader was talking earnestly to the other two of her athletes. Realizing that something had distracted them from her instructions, she turned and followed their gaze. When she saw Luke, her face darkened.

She shouted, "Hey! I was promised that I could train my people behind closed doors."

"Sorry," Luke called down to her. "Doors aren't closed to an FI. But don't worry. I'm not after your coaching secrets."

"Are we being investigated?" the trainer asked, clearly vexed.

"No. I'm just looking around. More interested in the building."

She didn't reply. With her hands on her hips and a frown on her face, she waited.

Luke didn't expect to gain anything from his visit. He was simply familiarizing himself with the area. "This place hasn't suffered any damage, has it?"

The coach shook her head. It was a sign of impatience and not an answer. "How should I know? I reserve it for sessions, that's all. It has what I need. I don't care about anything else. But if I can't have it to myself, I'm taking my team away. Right now."

Surprised by her bad mood, Luke shrugged. "No need. I'll leave you to it."

Chapter Eight

Luke pulled his coat around him as he sat in the small covered area to the side of one of the training fields. Above him, a long line of pigeons had settled side by side on the overhang. Two wiry long-distance runners were jogging around and around the track alongside each other. This time there was no hostility, no protest at Luke's presence. When the girls ran past, effortlessly matching their strides, they both smiled and nodded toward him. Luke called "Hi" and wished he could join them.

Instead, he said to Malc, "There's no chance of Spoilsport being one of Owen's athletes. They might wish that they could have some events in the dome, but it didn't exist as a sports venue when Spoilsport meddled with the plane a couple of years ago. So, no motive."

"That is valid reasoning, as long as all acts of sabotage have been carried out by one person."

"I'm following the simplest theory first. I'm going to assume that it's down to a single person until I see something that tells me I'm wrong."

"That is the correct approach."

"Thanks," Luke muttered with a smile. "Just out of interest, who was that grumpy trainer in the gym? Can you access reservations?"

"Searching."

Luke watched the runners for a while. One of them kept glancing at her watch and muttering something—probably their lap times—to her companion.

"The practice gymnasium is reserved today in the name of Yvonne Chaplow," Malc announced.

"I wonder why she was so touchy. Does she have any good athletes?"

There was a loud thump from a nearby construction site, and the pigeons all took off together.

Malc answered, "Yvonne Chaplow is an expert on muscle movement. She coaches athletes from a wide variety of disciplines that require specific muscle groups and posture to be optimized. This includes rowers, skaters, soccer players, marathon runners, and gymnasts. Several are being considered for the Games. For example, Ford Drayton has recently emerged as a contender for the marathon, and Saskia Frame is a fourteen-year-old gymnast."

"She'd have no trouble climbing up scaffolding and swinging on railings," Luke said with a grin. Thinking of the gymnast's ill-tempered coach again, he added, "It's tempting to put Yvonne Chaplow on my list of suspects because she was horrible, but you'll tell me that getting revenge isn't a legally valid approach. You'll want a motive."

"She has a motive. According to records, she is not in favor of regenerating Hounslow. She believes that the

Games should be held in a northern center of sporting excellence with existing facilities and an outstanding reputation for gymnastics."

"Mmm. So she might want to see Hounslow fail. While we're on the topic of suspects, Malc, open that file on objectors to the development. The one with Frank Russell in it. How many others are in there?"

"Three."

"Tell me about them."

"Holly Queenan," Malc told him, "is probably twenty-four years old. Little is known about her. My records indicate that she has two convictions for theft. William Underwood is a seventy-eight-year-old biologist living in Ealing. Currently, he is sick, and medical files suggest that he is nearing the end of his life."

Luke interrupted. "Is he the one Frank Russell told us about? His neighbor with a reptile house?"

"Insufficient data, but highly likely."

"Who's the other protester?"

"A historian named Trevor Twigg. He is thirty-one years old."

"All right. I'll need to speak to them all. Better start with William Underwood, but he's not Spoilsport if he's really sick."

The old man's voice called, "Is that you, Elsie?"

William's young nurse touched her patient's arm. "No.

It's a forensic investigator." She turned to Luke and whispered, "Elsie's his wife. Died two years ago, after fifty-six years together. It's terrible what Hounslow's done to him." She shook her head sadly. "I'll leave you to it."

Luke sat beside the old man's bed, and Malc perched on a sideboard.

William's head on the pillow looked like a disheveled bird in a nest. He turned toward his visitor and said, "The hospital sent me home to die. Not much of a home. This is my new place. Not a patch on . . ." His eyes lost focus for a moment, and he looked puzzled. "We got evicted. The move was too much for her."

"Who?"

"Elsie."

"I'm sorry," Luke replied. "What do you remember of your old place in Hounslow?"

"Bernard got hold of one of Frank's young pigeons." Suddenly, surprising Luke, he burst out laughing. It was more of an unearthly cackle really.

"Who's Bernard?"

"My Nile monitor lizard. He'd enjoy a baby pigeon. Delicious. Frank was livid." He laughed again. "Elsie didn't like the horned lizard."

Trying to keep him talkative, Luke asked, "Why not?"

"Didn't like the blood."

"What?"

"It squirts blood from its eyes when it's under threat.

66

A quarter of its blood flies out."

Grimacing, Luke didn't know what to say. He didn't know whether to believe the confused old man, either. He turned to look at Malc.

His mobile said, "That is a correct description of the horned lizard's defense mechanism. The foul-tasting blood comes from sinuses behind the eyes."

"Charming." Luke looked back at William. "What happened to your reptile house?"

All humor vanished from his face. "Flattened."

"And the animals?"

"A vet was on his way to collect them, but the bulldozer got there first. Frank's pigeons could fly away, but not Bernard and the rest of mine. All gone." William's eyes became wet with tears.

The reptiles' fate was a shame, Luke knew, and the memory had remained clear in William's fogged brain, but it didn't seem to have anything to do with his inquiry. "Did you get along well with Frank?"

The old man nodded weakly. "Wanted us to join his fight. But . . . there was Elsie to think of . . ." He ran out of words.

To prevent him from getting more distressed, Luke asked, "What about Holly Queenan and Trevor Twigg? Do you know them?"

William seemed to be gazing at something beyond the ceiling. "No."

"Was anyone else fighting against the development?"

"I don't . . ." He twisted his head to look at Luke. "How could they do that to Elsie and my pets?"

Luke shrugged. "It should've been handled better."

"You're young," William said, as if he'd just noticed Luke's age. At once, though, his mind drifted. "There are rats in here. They say that there aren't, but I've seen them. Big ones. Didn't have rats before. My snakes would've swallowed them whole. You should've tasted Frank's strawberries. Or was it blueberries?"

Luke smiled. "I bet Frank's a lot healthier than he looks. Is that right?"

"Frank? He's strong. Stronger than me. Put it down to digging his garden. Always on the go. He kept pigeons as well."

"Did he use chemicals? On his garden, not his pigeons."

"I don't think so. But . . ." He shrugged helplessly.

"Did either of you work for the airport?"

"The airport?" William looked shocked. "We would rather die."

"Did you hear about the plane crash?"

William looked puzzled. "What plane crash?"

"Two years ago."

"That was when Elsie . . ."

"Yes," Luke said softly.

"No," William replied. "I can't remember a plane crash. It was grief that took my Elsie."

Thinking of the shotgun that blew up in its owner's hands, Luke asked, "Was there anyone who knew all about rifles?"

"Rifles? You don't want to mess around with that sort of thing. Dangerous."

"Yes, but do you remember anyone who did?"

He shook his head.

The door opened, and his home nurse came back in with a razor and a bowl of soapy water.

William craned his neck and called, "Is that you, Elsie?"

On his way back to Hounslow Residential, Luke stopped by the indoor arena and golf house. There were four large concrete pillars and, in front of them, a plinth, ready to take a statue of some sort. It would probably be a celebration of the human form, Luke guessed, in the shape of an athlete. The pillars were fancy, but the plinth was plain. Luke imagined that the designer didn't want an ornate base to detract from the sculpture still to come.

"This is the last thing Libby Byrne worked on," Luke said, reaching out and touching the rough pedestal. Struck by a chilling thought, he shuddered and glanced at Malc. "Can any of your scans penetrate concrete?"

"Only to a few inches, depending on the density of the matrix."

"Is there anything that can look all the way through?"

"Confirmed."

"Order it, Malc. I want to see if there's anything inside the pillars and the plinth aside from concrete. Like Libby Byrne's body."

"Transmitting request."

Chapter Nine

It was Friday evening. Luke had stripped down to a T-shirt because his room was sweltering. The thermostat had clearly gone wrong, but at least there was no shortage of electricity. Luke was occupied with the horrifying thought that Libby could have ended up encased in concrete, until he was interrupted by a vibration that seemed to bore right into his head. Somewhere below him, a decorator was drilling into the wall. Unaffected by the irritating noise, Malc said, "The kitchen has informed me that your dinner is ready."

"Thanks. Ask them to bring it up and come straight in. Unlock the door. That's fine."

"Sending message."

Luke had only been on the Spoilsport case for two full days, but already he was feeling frustrated. "It's one thing to come up with a few promising motives and people who had the opportunity, but getting real evidence is going to be tricky on a huge, filthy building site."

"To gain a conviction, eyewitness statements or confessions must be supported by some physical evidence."

"Thanks for giving me a Year-8 criminology lesson, Malc."

"Gratitude is unnecessary."

"The thing that's bothering me the most is Libby Byrne. She could be in danger or dead. I need to find her

one way or another. Top priority. And I want to know why her partner's heart rate went up when I asked him about the Games."

"You should also interview the objectors, Holly Queenan and Trevor Twigg. However, Holly Queenan's whereabouts are unknown."

Behind them, the door slid open, and a female voice said, "Room service. Dinner for Forensic Investigator Harding."

At once, Luke gasped and spun around.

"Hiya!" Hardly able to suppress her laughter, Jade wheeled the trolley into Luke's room.

"What . . . ?" Dumbstruck, Luke's stood open-mouthed in amazement.

"How's things?"

"It's . . . you." Luke jumped to his feet.

Jade looked into the mirror to her right. "True."

It took Luke another second to understand. Then he exclaimed, "You got the anthem job! You didn't tell me!"

"What? And miss the opportunity to see that wide-eyed expression when I came in?"

Luke ran to her. "But . . . you don't come down south."

"I made an exception for the Games' music," she replied, throwing her arms around him.

"Brilliant," Luke said. "Well done." Towering above her, he glanced down at the trolley. "Did you bribe your way into the job by agreeing to deliver room services?"

She giggled. "I hope you're hungry."

Luke nodded.

"Me too. I got them to make lots for both of us." She unwrapped her arms from around him and added, "Seems like they'll do anything for the Games' musician. Look." She took away one of the lids to reveal a plate of fruits.

"What's this?" Luke said in amazement.

"Well, I thought you'd be able to tell me, you being an expert and an investigator. If you're not sure, see if Malc can recognize it."

"It's a pomegranate!"

"Your favorite. Ten out of ten."

"Huh. Nothing was happening for me. Malc set up a supply from Jordan, but the kitchen wasn't getting its act sorted out at this end. How come you . . . ?"

"I asked nicely before I set out. I said the Games' musician needed them, and . . ." She shrugged. "That was that. They'll be on the breakfast menu while I'm here."

A small lizard, off-white with gray bands and light pink on its head and legs, ran down the wall, across the floor, and disappeared into one of the heating vents.

Surprised, Luke said, "What was that? And what's it doing here?"

"It is a reptile of the family Gekkonidae," Malc answered. "It is widespread in warm climates. It is probably searching for spiders to eat."

For a moment, Luke was back on the case. He said,

"I wonder if it's one of William Underwood's pets. One that escaped from the bulldozer and is now living in the nice, warm ventilation system." He looked at Jade and said, "I bet your room doesn't come with lizards and spiders. You've probably got staff to shoo them away for you."

"That's right," she said. "I've got my own creepy-crawly warden, a hairdresser, a girl who puts toothpaste on my toothbrush, another one who flushes my toilet, and my personal chef."

"Huh. If I were you, I'd keep the last two far apart. Are you still going to complain about how awful everything is in the South?"

More serious this time, Jade replied, "Outside of this sports scheme, yes. I saw what it's like from the cab on the way down here. But we're hungry. Let's start before it gets cold."

"It doesn't matter, does it?" Luke replied. "You can call in your personal food reheating attendant."

"Very funny," said Jade.

At 6:30 on Saturday morning, Luke met Jade downstairs in the reception area of the accommodation block. Bleary-eyed, Luke said, "Are you sure this is a good idea?" He'd promised to take her to the main stadium while it was still dark, before the builders began their day's work and before her official guide arrived.

Always full of life, Jade rarely looked tired. "Yes," she replied enthusiastically. "I want to see the sun rising over the stadium. It's symbolic. Dawn's a new beginning, like the regeneration itself, like the opening of the Games. They're all the start of something big. I'm hoping daybreak'll give me inspiration."

Luke didn't pretend to understand, but he said, "All right." He would have preferred to stay in bed, but, trying to be cheerful, he added, "I've always wanted to see what you look like in a hard hat."

It wasn't an improvement. She stood beside the control room, her head swamped by the protective hat, and took in the scale of the place as daylight began to flood the stadium. "Wow," she said. "It's huge. Just the positioning and type of speakers is going to be . . . a challenge."

Overhead, a suspended platform let out a creak. Luke glanced upward nervously, but there was no sign of movement. He hoped that the noise was normal when the sun's rays began to warm and expand the metalwork.

"Plans and photos will remind me when I'm back in Sheffield," Jade said, "but there's nothing like being here, soaking in the atmosphere."

Luke looked around the empty stadium as well, wishing that he could also be inspired. He needed something special to solve his case. The sun was low in the sky and bright enough to sting his eyes, yet there was

a winter chill in the air. His hands ached from the cold.

"I want to bathe the whole space in sound," Jade said, looking up at the enormous arch and the oval canopy, "so everyone gets the same experience, whether they're on the field or at the back of one of the stands. Tricky, but putting a bank of downward-facing speakers in the overhang might be the answer—like floodlighting but with sound."

Luke thought that he heard a sound behind them. A bump. He spun around. There was nothing but the control room, filled with an array of computers and monitors. Most of them had not yet been fully installed.

Jade glanced at him. "You're twitchy this morning."

"Yes, well. Somewhere, there's someone—Spoilsport—trying to make sure that the Games won't happen." He turned to Malc and asked, "Did you hear a noise?"

"Confirmed. In the last few seconds, I have logged twelve types of sounds."

"Aside from us speaking, the place creaking, and anything normal. It might have come from the control room." He took a few steps toward its broad window.

"I have recorded one thud from that direction."

Luke cupped both hands around his eyes to cut out the sun's glare that was reflecting off the glass and peered into the room.

Almost at once, the side door opened, and a shadowy figure took off at high speed toward the main exit. The faded jeans, scuffed fleece coat, and hood told Luke that it wasn't a builder. All construction workers wore overalls and a hard hat. Luke did not see the intruder's face. But something about the running style told him that it was a woman. "Stop!" he shouted. "Forensic Investigator!"

But she didn't hesitate.

Luke said, "Pursue, Malc. Don't hurt her, though. Obstruct mode only. And call in security guards." He glanced at Jade and said, "Hang on here." Then he sprinted along the gap between the rows of seats, chasing the prowler who had broken into the control room.

Chapter Ten

Luke lost sight of Malc because he was concentrating on hurrying down the stone steps without falling. Some way in front of him, the intruder was equally nimble on her feet. But Luke was confident that, with or without Malc's help, he'd catch her. He believed that he could outrun her, unless she was a contender for the International Youth Games. He was also hoping that arresting Spoilsport had become as straightforward as winning this race.

He reached the bottom of the steps and, stretching his long legs, accelerated along the passageway. Ahead of him in the wide tunnel, the woman was sprinting for the exit. Now that it was a straight race, with piles of rubble as the only obstacles, Luke began gaining on her. She would emerge into the open air first, though. He had to trust that Malc would be on hand to track her, in case she tried to lose Luke in the countless pathways through the construction site.

Reaching the open air, the woman skidded to a halt. Malc was hovering at the entrance in obstruct mode. As a warning, he shot a bright-red laser beam from his underside and hit the concrete floor a few inches in front of the woman.

Luke slowed down to a walk as she glanced fearfully at him over her shoulder. "You're trapped," Luke called. "Don't do anything silly that'd make things worse for you. I don't want to tell Malc to go into attack mode, and you don't want to be charged with resisting arrest as well."

Her hood still obscuring her face, the woman looked at Luke and then at Malc. Then her shoulders drooped and she sighed. "All right."

"Who are you?" Luke asked, holding out his identity card. "Take your hood off, please."

Resigned, she flicked it back, revealing a woman in her mid-twenties. But she didn't speak.

"Have you got an identity card?"

"What do you think?" she muttered.

Luke stayed around six feet away from her. If she produced a weapon and tried to assault him, Malc would stop her before she could harm him. "Hold up your hands so that my mobile can scan your fingerprints."

She began to lift her arms, but instead of displaying her palms, she darted away.

Still not wanting to upgrade Malc's status, Luke dived at her and flung his arms around her shins. He brought her down with a perfect rugby tackle. Pressing his knee into her back and pinning her down, he said, "Final warning. Do that again, and I'll put my mobile on to you. Then, when you go down, you won't get up again in a

79

hurry. Now, I'm going to let you up, and I want your hands in the air for a scan."

When Luke scrambled to his feet, she did as she was told.

Trying to catch her off-guard, Luke asked, "What have you done with Libby Byrne?"

"Who? I haven't done anything to anyone."

"Are you carrying a weapon?"

"No."

Realizing that he was dealing with someone slippery, Luke said, "Malc? Scan for weapons."

"There is a knife in a holster around the shoulder."

Luke shook his head. "Throw it down," he said to her.

Muttering to herself, she yanked it out and dropped it unwillingly onto the floor.

"Kick it away."

The knife clattered across the bare concrete.

"I'm not in a good mood," said Luke. "I haven't even had breakfast yet. So tell me the truth from now on. What were you doing in the stadium?"

"What do you think?" she repeated.

"I could guess all sorts of things. Some very serious. You'd better just tell me."

Malc interrupted. "I have an identity confirmed through facial recognition and fingerprint comparison with criminal files. This is Holly Queenan."

"Ah," Luke said. "I've been wanting to talk to you."

She sniffed. "Why?" she asked.

"Because you used to live here. You got kicked out to make way for the Games."

"So?"

"You must be angry."

"It was all right around here. Now . . ." She shrugged. "Hopeless."

Luke nodded. "I get it. You're saying it was easy for a bandit before. Good hunting ground."

She stared at Luke without saying a word.

"Yes, I know about your record. Two convictions for theft."

"I was one of a local gang. That's all. And this was our patch. The others moved away. Scattered. I like it here, so I stayed."

"Stealing brand-new computers from the sports stadium."

She didn't deny it.

"What else were you up to?"

"Look. Just arrest me, if that's what you're going to do."

Four guards came to a halt outside of the sports stadium. Luke called out to them, "It's okay. Everything's under control. But stay around. I'll want you to take her away to a holding cell in a minute." He turned back to Holly and said, "Have you done anything else in the control room?"

"Like what?" she snapped.

"You might've interfered with it in some way."

She shook her head. "Not my style."

Talking to Malc, Luke said, "Do her prints match anything in the swimming pool?"

"No," Malc answered.

"What's paraquat?" Luke asked her.

"Don't ask me."

Malc intervened. "You cannot order a forensic investigator to leave out a question."

"No, Malc. She answered. She means she doesn't know what paraquat is." He gazed at Holly and continued, "I can already arrest you for trespassing. When I go back into the control room, your fingerprints will be all over at least one computer. That'll be attempted theft as well."

"What are you waiting for, then?"

Some builders arrived and gathered together in a group, eager to start work inside. One of them shouted, "Did she do it? Is she the killer?" Another called, "What's she done now? Is it safe?"

Luke gazed at Holly and raised his eyebrows. "Well? Have you sabotaged anything?"

Wary of the group of restless builders, Holly looked distraught rather than defiant. "That wasn't me! I don't . . . No. You can't get me for that. I just wanted a computer."

"Mmm."

It was turning into a circus. Neil Gladwin, the site manager, ran up to the stadium entrance and gasped,

"What's going on? Have you got her?"

Behind Luke, Jade arrived and muttered, "Is it always as exciting as this?"

Trying to defuse the situation, Luke said to Holly, "I have sufficient evidence to charge you with trespassing and attempted theft." Then he signaled for the guards to take her away while he had a quiet conversation with Neil. "You might want to send a team in to check that everything's okay before you open it up for work. Just in case. I found her in the control room. That's probably the place to start. But I don't really think that she's your saboteur."

Neil seemed reluctant to accept Luke's opinion. He was desperate to blame someone for the sabotage. "If you lock her away and everything settles down—no more incidents—you'll have to change your mind."

Luke smiled. "Maybe."

"By the way, I've just received a request to bring some sort of specialized scanner on site. Apparently, you asked for it."

Malc replied, "I have already given permission. The scanner will be delivered to the indoor sports arena in an estimated thirty minutes."

Neil frowned. "What on earth are you doing with it?"

"I'm going to scan the front of the building. If it throws anything up," Luke replied evasively, "I'll let you know."

"Well, be careful in and around the arena this morning.

There's an infestation of rats, and a controller's coming in today to get rid of them."

On the way back to the apartment block, Jade nudged Luke and said, "Go on. Tell me. What's this secret scanner for?"

Luke screwed up his face. "You don't want to know."

"It's something to do with a body, then."

Luke nodded.

"It's probably gruesome."

"Sure is."

She shivered. "In that case, you're right. I don't want to know."

Chapter Eleven

When Jade left for a tour of Hounslow with her official guide and bodyguard, Luke walked to the indoor arena. He was troubled by the idea that Libby Byrne could have been knocked unconscious or drugged early on Monday and placed inside of one of the molds outside of the grand entrance. Unknowingly, a builder could have poured wet concrete over her later in the day. Worst of all, Luke wondered if she might have woken up to witness her own burial. He shuddered and cursed his imagination. It would have been an awful death. Fully conscious, she would have died of asphyxiation before the concrete solidified around her.

Like Malc, the scanner could sustain its own weight by hovering. It was slightly smaller than a Mobile Aid to Law and Crime, but while Malc had multiple functions, the device was dedicated to the task of scanning dense solids. Like an X-ray machine probing through skin and tissue to to see the underlying bone, the scanner could search for anything in the interior that was unlike the rest.

"All right," Luke said with a sigh. "Let's get it over with. Program it to check the entire height of the first pillar. I'm looking for a discontinuity inside. Something about the size and shape of a human being."

The unit spiraled very slowly up the pillar, downloading the data directly into Malc.

Luke wasn't the only person standing there, studying the scanner's progress. A man carrying a large duffel bag stopped on the steps and, shielding his eyes from the sun, watched what was going on. Obviously curious, he approached Luke and asked, "What's that? What's happening?"

"Who are you?"

The man held out his identity card. "Ian Pritchard. Vet. Sadly, not curing anything today. They want me to exterminate their rats."

Luke nodded. "Yes, the site manager told me." He waved a hand toward the scanner and said, "I'm just looking for faults in the structure."

"Faults?" Ian seemed alarmed. "Is it safe for me to go in? You can't be too careful, can you? Not with . . . everything that's going on around here."

Luke smiled. "No. It's fine. Not that sort of fault."

"Good. Thanks." As he headed toward the door, Ian glanced once more at the scanner as it lowered itself to the ground.

Malc announced, "No irregularities detected."

"Try the next one. And keep going if it doesn't spot anything. All four pillars and then the plinth."

Really, Luke should have set it to work on the pedestal first. It was broader than the pillars, and it seemed more likely to provide a permanent hiding place for a body. Being less well made, there was even a chance that an amateur—like Spoilsport—had poured the concrete in. But Luke was dreading a positive result. He was putting it off as long as possible by asking for scans of the ornate pillars first.

He couldn't avoid it indefinitely, though. When the machine drew a blank on all four pillars, it moved to the plinth, and Luke held his breath.

Because the base was squat, the examination did not take long. Within a couple of minutes, Malc announced, "There are two pockets within the structure. One measures nine cubic inches, and the other is eighteen cubic inches. They are probably composed of air, and they are much too small to conceal significant parts of a human being."

"Nothing else?"

"Confirmed."

Luke felt relieved. His worst fear had come to nothing. But he felt thwarted as well because a good theory had also come to nothing. "Okay. At least I know where Libby isn't. You can get an agent to take the scanner away. I've finished with it." For a moment, he stood outside the arena and thought about his next move. Then he said to Malc, "Come on. I'm going inside. I want a quick word with that vet."

"It is not possible to conduct an interview using a single word, irrespective of the speed of delivery."

"Right. By the time I've found him," Luke said, going up the steps two at a time, "I'll have thought of some whole sentences with a bit of luck."

Luke discovered Ian Pritchard crouching in the corner of a pool room with his arm poking down into a hole between the floorboards and the wall. He was making a tut-tutting noise with his tongue.

"How's it going?" Luke asked.

Ian yanked his arm out and dusted himself down while shaking his head. "I've put a bowl of poison down there, and it'll kill a few, but . . ." He sighed. "While the place is still in this state—convenient little holes everywhere and the builders leaving half-eaten sandwiches around—there's no hope. It's a rat magnet. I'll take care of one lot and then the next'll move in." He held up a clear plastic bag containing two dead, mangy rats. "You know what got these, don't you? They love electric cables. They like chewing the plastic insulation. These two sunk their teeth in too deep, contacted the live wire, and electrocuted themselves."

Luke was unable to muster much sympathy for the disease-ridden pests. "Saves you the effort," he replied.

"I suppose so." He tied the bag and dropped it into his duffel bag. "Not the nicest of this earth's creatures, are they?"

Really, Luke wanted to talk to him about William Underwood, and he spotted the opportunity. "Not many keep them as pets. I know an old Hounslow man who used to have his own reptile house. He kept an interesting selection of snakes and lizards. Even gave them names." He let out a little laugh. "Do you know him?"

Ian shook his head. "I don't think so."

"He was named William, and he asked for a vet to help him with them when the builders moved in."

"Hang on a minute," Ian said, getting to his feet. "Was this out near the runway?"

"A couple of years ago. Yes."

He began to nod slowly. "A long time. I'd forgotten. I suppose I've done a lot since then. Anyway, yes. That was me. He called me out, but by the time I got there, the place was being flattened. Terrible. He was distraught, as I remember. Like he'd lost his partner. Poor old chap."

"Poor old reptiles as well."

"Yes. A few would have survived, I guess. The bulldozer would have gotten most of them. The weather would've killed quite a few survivors. The rest might've adapted."

"How was William Underwood, aside from distraught?"

"What do you mean?"

Luke shrugged. "Was he healthy and well, sick, angry maybe?"

"Angry, yes. Very. Threatening all kinds of things, he was. I don't remember him being sick, but he wasn't exactly a youngster. It was his partner who was unwell, wasn't it?"

"Elsie."

Ian shook his head. "I can't remember names. And

certainly not the names of his reptiles."

Luke's spine was tingling. "When you say he was threatening all kinds of things, what do you mean? What sort of things?"

The vet let out a long breath. "I'm not sure. He was ranting and raving. He definitely talked about flattening the site manager to see how he liked it. Or was it a she? Anyway, he was all for getting revenge by pulling their buildings down on them." He stopped and smiled wryly. "We all say things like that when we're upset, don't we? That's what a shock does to us, isn't it? He didn't really mean it. At least, I don't think he did."

"Thanks," Luke replied. "That's helpful."

As soon as he was outside, Luke said to his mobile, "Urgent task, Malc. I want to know if anyone was due to take the plane that crashed but didn't turn up for it. In other words, search for an original passenger list, not the actual list of people who flew."

"Task logged."

"And I think it's time that I talked to Trevor Twigg, the historian. With a bit of luck, he'll be at home on a Saturday. Plot me a route."

"Complying."

The rickety pier stretched out over the dull, gray English Channel. There had been two huts halfway along the weather-beaten jetty, but one month ago a tsunami had demolished them in seconds. Now the pier was reduced to a long line of wooden slats—and some of those were missing. The far end had collapsed into the sea. Only the most daring anglers still picked their way along the sea-scarred structure to a good fishing point.

Luke stood at the entry to Brighton Pier, on the last bit of firm ground, and watched two distant fishermen holding their rods against the warped railing. "Well, according to his partner, Trevor's one of them," Luke said. "And it's too cold to wait." He looked down at the pier, groaned, and stepped onto the first plank. "If it's safe enough for them, it's safe enough for me."

"Illogical," Malc replied. "A forensic investigator is more valuable."

Luke laughed as he set out along the jetty. "Just scan ahead and tell me if you detect any weak points."

Through the gaps between slats, Luke glimpsed waves churning up sand below him. A bitter wind was turning the restless sea into spray. It felt like rain, but the water on his face tasted salty. Treading carefully, making sure that he stepped over the missing boards, he reached the first fisherman and asked, "Are you Trevor Twigg?"

The man nodded. "I'm still allowed to fish here, aren't I?"

Luke held out his identity card in a gloved hand. "No idea. I think it should be banned myself. Much too cold. Maybe in the summer."

"What are you here for, then?" Trevor asked.

"I want to talk to you about Hounslow."

"Ah. Hounslow." An expression of sadness and resentment flashed across his face, reddened by the cold wind.

"You made yourself a nuisance," said Luke.

"Nonsense. I wasn't the nuisance. That was the developers. I just resisted a silly initiative."

"Why silly?"

"More destructive than silly." Trevor shuffled the fishing rod in his hands. "You might think that I'm crazy, but I liked the old Hounslow. And I like it here in Brighton. People should appreciate the imperfect. Much more interesting than the spotless. You see, places in the South have a feeling of being lived in, a real sense of history. They've seen so much. Restoring and preserving Hounslow would've been better than sweeping it away. Such a pity. It needed tender loving care, not demolishing and starting again."

"Have you been back?"

"Now and again. I can't resist taking a look at what they're doing. Crazy."

Luke glanced down at a spare rod and tackle, a plastic tub of squirming worms, and two cod lying on tinfoil close to his feet.

"Dinner tonight and breakfast in the morning," Trevor said. "Fish doesn't get fresher than that."

"Do you know Libby Byrne?"

"Site manager. Vandal-in-chief." He kept his gaze on the sea. When he wound in his line a little, his hand was shaking. He was either nervous or cold.

"Do you know what's happened to her?"

"No."

Luke thought it was odd that Trevor didn't ask what had prompted the question. Maybe he knew but wouldn't admit it. "What's paraquat?"

Trevor glanced at him with a frown that transformed into a smile. "Is this a chemistry lesson all of a sudden? It's a weed killer."

"What exactly was your problem with the regeneration?"

"Regeneration! As if there was only one era worth regenerating. I applied for an archaeological dig. I wanted to regenerate a past way of life, to unearth the stories of people who lived there throughout the ages. We could have learned a lot, instead of burying it and losing the record forever. But you know what they said? Not enough time! I got turned down because there wasn't time before the Games. Ridiculous. It's never a waste of time to study a time line. By now, we could've been on the way to conserving and logging our past, followed by a sensitive modernization, blended with the best of what was already there."

"You didn't stay, though," Luke pointed out. "You moved here."

"People got rehoused in all sorts of places. Some locally, but a lot went to Birmingham or Leeds. They jumped at the chance. Well, most would, wouldn't they? Not me, though. But I gave up protesting when the damage was done, when bulldozers and new buildings ruined it all." He paused and looked at Luke. "I'm not a forensic investigator, but I expect that you'd feel the same if someone leveled a crime scene and then dumped a load of concrete over it. There's no point in carrying on after the slate's been wiped clean. I couldn't live so close to that sort of vandalism."

"Where were you first thing on Monday morning?"

"Here," Trevor answered right away, as if he was expecting Luke's question. "The start of my week's fishing trip."

"Was anyone with you?"

"No."

"So there's no one to vouch for you," said Luke.

"No."

Again, Luke was suspicious because the historian didn't ask why he was interested in the beginning of the week.

Trevor began to reel in his next catch. It looked effortless. "Cod aren't like me. They're not known for putting up a fight." His serious expression suggested that there was a particular significance in what he was saying. "I guess you'd like to catch whoever you're after without a fight as well. But . . ." He hesitated as he lifted the limp cod out of the water. "Most fish are a lot harder to land.

They're cunning and tough. You could have a big battle on your hands, like dragging up a skate."

His words sounded like a challenge.

Chapter Twelve

In the electric cab speeding toward Hounslow, Malc reported, "I have obtained the original passenger list for Flight GGW17."

"Good. Compare it with the list of people who actually flew. Are there any differences?"

"Yes."

"What are they, then?"

"Libby Byrne intended to take Flight GGW17 but did not check in."

Luke nodded and smiled. "Thought so." Pleased with himself, he explained, "That vet said William Underwood threatened to get revenge on Libby Byrne. I know it's only hearsay, but it sounded like he would've happily brought her new buildings down on her. Well, okay, a plane isn't a building, but it was part of the regeneration. Libby was due to take the flight, and it was brought down. That's some coincidence. Meaning, it probably wasn't a coincidence. It was an attempt to kill Libby—and undermine the regeneration scheme. But William can't be Spoilsport. He can hardly get out of bed, not to mention climb a lot of ladders." As the cab powered toward London, an increasing wind sent heavy clouds racing across the sky. The windows became spotted with raindrops, distorting Luke's view. "I'm more suspicious about Trevor Twigg, but there's not much I can do without evidence." Luke let out a long sigh.

When the computerized cab slowed down and stopped at the Hounslow terminus, Luke and Malc got out. Lingering at the spot, Luke watched the electric vehicle swing around the loop and leave the development site. He turned up his collar against the wind and rain. "This is where the builders arrive for work, including Libby Byrne, I guess. Unless she was taken from outside of her own house or went somewhere without telling anyone." He turned to Malc and said, "Scan for Libby's brown briefcase, thirty feet on either side of the track, please."

A large, empty plastic bag hurtled down the cab corridor like a sail and slapped against an idle bulldozer.

Late on a Saturday afternoon, the place was much quieter than normal. Luke tried to picture the scene on Monday morning. If Libby took a cab—as Royston suggested—she would have gotten out here. But she never reached her headquarters around 1,200 feet away. Luke feared for her. If he was right that the downing of Flight GGW17 was a first attempt to murder Libby, it seemed likely that there'd been a second attempt at the beginning of the week. And because she hadn't surfaced, he suspected that it had been successful.

There was another possibility, though. Luke's mind went back to a boy at school who, whenever he struggled

with a piece of work, faked an illness or claimed that his project had been erased by a programming bug or a computer virus. Luke wondered if Libby Byrne was so overwhelmed by her job that she'd figured out a way to blame someone else for any failure. He wondered if, all along, she'd been looking for a way out. Maybe she'd sabotaged Flight GGW17, booked a seat on it, and then deliberately missed it so that she appeared to be the intended victim, throwing suspicion elsewhere. Afterward, she'd begun undermining her own building project as an excuse for her inability to cope. That way, an unknown saboteur would take the blame for the delays. The idea was Luke's most fanciful theory, but it wasn't beyond his imagination. And if Libby Byrne was Spoilsport, she had gone underground.

Either way, Luke knew that he had to find Libby. Dead or alive. Victim or culprit.

"My scan has failed to detect a briefcase within the stated parameters," Malc said.

"All right. Continue scanning thirty feet on either side of the walkway between here and the manager's headquarters. I want you to find anything that might've belonged to Libby Byrne."

Rain was sweeping almost horizontally across Hounslow. The dusty site was turning rapidly into a mud bath. A large roll of insulation material blew past Malc, unraveling comically as it went. With the storm and the approach of sunset, there wasn't a lot of light, but unlike Luke, Malc did not need it to complete a search.

Malc was also undaunted by the lashing rain, but Luke was getting drenched. After a while, with his hair flattened against his head and cold water trickling unpleasantly down his neck, he yelled, "I'm taking cover." He pointed to a new small building like a bunker that was destined to become secure storage for equipment. "In there."

He dashed inside before he heard Malc's warning.

By the long fluorescent light in the ceiling, Luke saw right away what Malc was about to tell him. There was a young woman in the corner of the room, peering into her cupped hands with a concerned expression on her face. Because she was looking down, Luke didn't recognize her immediately.

The woman jumped in shock at the sudden appearance of a forensic investigator and Mobile Aid to Law and Crime. "Oh," she said. "It's you."

Luke wiped the water from his hair and face with cold hands. "What are you doing here?" he asked William Underwood's nurse.

"Nothing," she answered. Then she smiled at her absurd reply. "Well, not nothing, obviously. Sheltering."

"Mmm. What else?"

"Look. I know this'll sound stupid, but . . ."

"What?"

"It's my day off, and I'm looking for lizards. You see, if I could find just one or two of William's pets . . . well, it'd mean so much to him. He'd die happy then."

Her explanation was so ridiculous that Luke believed her. She certainly wouldn't have invented something like that. "Did he send you out to do any other favors for him?"

"No. What do you mean?"

Shaking the rainwater from his hands, Luke pretended to be more concerned with his own comfort than the possibility of a sympathetic nurse carrying out William's threats against the regeneration. "He might've asked you to do a few things that he can't manage himself anymore, far beyond what a home nurse usually does."

She shook her head as if she didn't really understand what he meant.

When the storage room was finished, there would be sealed cabinets for shotguns, pistols, and ammunition. Archery bows and javelins would be kept in open racks, and arrows would be bunched together in numerous quivers. Luke nodded toward the nurse's hands, still clenched together. "What have you got there? A lizard? One of William's?"

"No. It's a frog. Sort of."

"Did he keep amphibians as well?"

"I don't think so. I was just getting out of the rain, and I saw it lurking in the corner. Nice and snug until I . . ." She raised her clasped hands slightly.

"You said, 'Sort of.' What does that mean?"

"Take a look if you like." She stepped toward Luke and opened up the improvised cage.

Squatting in her palms was a green and grumpy frog. Its eyes stared up at Luke as if it was confused, even pleading. In a way, the ailing animal reminded Luke of Brooke Adams after her swimming accident. Its skin was rough with black patches that were perfectly normal for a frog yet looked like sores. But the animal was a freak. Its left front leg was barely more than a stump. Worse, one short leg and two unnaturally long ones stuck out of its rear end. "Five legs," Luke muttered.

"Weird sizes as well," the nurse noted. "The poor thing's deformed. I don't know why, but I think it's frightened. I'll put it back. Then I'd better get going—despite the weather. It'll be dark soon." She seemed eager to get away from an investigator.

"Before you go . . ." Luke said. "What's your name?"

"Venetia," she replied as she knelt down to replace the frog partially under a tarpaulin in the corner. "Venetia Murray."

Making his tone sound vaguely menacing, Luke said, "See you soon."

Venetia stood up and glanced at Luke warily before slinging her bag over her shoulder and hurrying away.

Peering out through the empty doorway, Luke waited for a few minutes. "It might be easing a bit," he said.

"Let's get going again."

By the time they reached the large trailer that served as the site manager's headquarters, Malc had still not detected anything useful for tracing Libby Byrne. Luke blew a raindrop off his nose and said, "Another blank. I want to go and talk to Libby's partner again, but in this weather, I'll do it by telescreen from my nice, warm, dry room. Unless Hounslow Residential's had another hiccup, and the plumbing's pouring cold water all over the place."

"A nonliving object cannot experience a spasmodic, involuntary inhalation of air followed by the snap closure of the windpipe."

"Open dictionary, Malc. A hiccup means a glitch as well. You'd probably call it a technical malfunction."

Rain pattered down on Malc, flowed over his shiny metallic exterior as if he was some artistic water feature, and then trickled onto the increasingly squelchy ground. Without a trace of humor or humiliation in his synthetic voice, he said, "Entered."

The larger-than-life version of Royston Klein on Luke's wall looked bemused. "Why did Libby want to fly to Glasgow? That was more than a year ago." He shook his head. "I'm not sure. It might've been to consult with some big sports development up there. I might be wrong, but I think she said she could learn from their experience."

"Knowing what happened to that plane, I would've

thought that it would stick in your mind."

"Yes. Well, I think that was it."

Luke asked, "Who knew that she was taking the flight?"

"Neil—her deputy—because he had to stand in for her."

Luke nodded. "And you, of course."

"Obviously."

"But she missed the flight. Why?"

He shrugged. "Something came up at work, ruining her plans. Not for the first time. But I can't remember what."

"You don't really like the idea of the new Hounslow and the Games, do you?"

For a moment, Royston was taken aback by Luke's sudden shift. Then he looked surprised. "I told you. It must be good for the kids. So, no, you're wrong. I'm all for it."

"But you're not entirely looking forward to it, are you? You're anxious about it for some reason."

"You're too young, FI Harding. If you had a partner, you'd understand. If she was in charge of something as big as the regeneration scheme, you'd be anxious as well. If she was missing, you'd be worried sick."

Luke nodded, but he remained convinced that Royston Klein was hiding something.

Chapter Thirteen

Once Malc had confirmed that Jade was back in her room, Luke said, "Right. I'm going down to see her. You're staying here."

"I cannot comply."

Luke groaned at the prospect of another battle with his mobile. "It has nothing to do with the Spoilsport case. It has everything to do with eating. You don't need meals. I do."

"Irrelevant. I must accompany you because you are in danger."

"Am I?"

"Confirmed. Spoilsport is likely to know that you are investigating the sabotage. You may have already interviewed him or her. Therefore, Spoilsport will regard you as a threat. As a result, you may be his or her next target."

"Yeah," Luke replied, making it up as he went along, "but I have this theory about reptiles, so I need you to gather some data for me while I have dinner with Jade."

"I am multitasking. I can protect you while gathering data remotely."

"That's not what I have in mind." To get time alone with Jade, Luke was willing to cheat. Keeping a grin at bay, he said, "I want you to stay here and record any lizards going in and out of the heating vent."

Malc hesitated. "Explain why this task has a higher priority than protecting you."

Luke shrugged. "I don't suppose it does, generally speaking. But I'm only going downstairs to a friend's room. I'm not even leaving the building. And I can't tell how important the lizard information is until you get it for me, but it has to do with William Underwood and his nurse. On top of that, I just need a break, Malc. I need a bit of space to myself."

"It is highly irregular."

"Okay. Here's a compromise. I go in to see Jade, and you wait outside the door. You can monitor lizards in the corridor instead and guard the room at the same time. I'll be safe that way."

"That is acceptable."

As soon as Luke went into Jade's suite, the scent hit him. He sniffed and frowned. "Phew. That's a powerful smell."

Jade laughed and pointed to a huge bouquet of flowers. "You've studied law. You must know the rule that says Games' musicians must get fresh flowers wherever they go. Perhaps someone thinks that it helps the creative spirit. I don't know. But I want to create breathtaking music that'll wither flowers at twenty paces. I want to see petals falling, or I haven't done my job properly."

"How did your tour of Hounslow go? Are you feeling inspired?"

"Maybe. It was . . . interesting. It's a big gig for me, you know. My pieces have to feel right in the sports venues, and they'll be booming out of every telescreen in every home watching the Games as well. Here and overseas. And in the corner of every telescreen there'll be a little credit to the composer. That's my name beaming out to millions. Scary."

"Jade. If you thought you weren't up to the job, what would you do?"

She looked aghast. "I am."

"Yeah. I know. I wasn't . . ." He started again. "Sorry. I was thinking about someone else, not you. I was thinking about a woman named Libby who might've taken on more than she could handle. I was wondering what you thought she'd do—blame someone else, run away, or what."

"Well, I know what I'd do. Admit it and resign. End of story. But maybe she's not honest like me."

"No. I think she'd want to save face."

Jade shrugged. "People can get pretty desperate, especially if they're trying to preserve their dignity. Didn't you take a course in psychology?"

"Criminal psychology, yes. This is different. Do you think a person would go as far as suicide or faking their own death?"

"If it's that important to them, yes. I can see someone driven that far. Sure."

"Mmm."

"Did you find your body—or whatever it was that you were looking for?"

"No." Trying to cheer both of them up, Luke said, "You didn't see a spare one lying around, did you?"

Jade giggled. "Not yet. But I am in the South. I'd expect to see a horrid one soon enough."

On the other side of the door, Malc patrolled the passageway, scanning for lizards, snakes, and a saboteur. Outside, a mixture of rain, hail, and snow slammed against the window. Unseen by Luke and Jade, the remaining conifer to the west of the building had begun to lurch. If the wind did not lessen soon, the tree would crash down on Hounslow Residential and Luke's room.

"I'm not an FI," Jade said, "but I think that you should release that girl you arrested."

"Holly Queenan?"

Jade nodded. "She's a local bandit. She knows this place inside out. A lot better than you do. If you get her trust, she'll tell you if she's seen anything."

"Maybe," Luke said, uncertainty clear in his voice. "And if she's Spoilsport, she'll create havoc when she's out."

Jade smiled and put her hand on his arm. "You don't think she's anything more than a thief. I can tell."

"True, but I'll leave it to you to convince Malc that she's off the suspect list."

"Ah. In that case, forget my advice," Jade said.

"I wish I had some sound for you to analyze in this case so you can be an assistant forensic investigator again. But . . ." Luke shrugged. "I don't."

"There's always another time."

"You might be too famous by then."

She laughed. "Never too famous to help a struggling FI."

"Thanks," he muttered sarcastically.

"Tell me, what do we do around here on a Saturday night? I didn't see any clubs or anything."

Luke shrugged. "You're not in Sheffield now. We eat and sleep. That's it."

Back in his own room, it wasn't easy to settle down. The storm growled, and somewhere near the roof, something was moving with a deep grating noise. It might have been tiles that were loosened by the wind. There was also a loud flapping sound, like a flag not just fluttering but shredding. In the middle of the night, reassured by Malc's faint flashing red light on the set of drawers and the starry night sky that he'd projected onto the ceiling, Luke closed his eyes and finally found sleep.

He was woken up a few minutes later by a massive clatter like an explosion. There was an icy blast through the room, and the air was thick with powdered plaster.

Broken tiles were raining down like stones, and pieces of glass from the window flew toward Luke like daggers. A thick branch came straight at him with lethal force. Dulled by sleepiness, Luke's reflexes were sluggish. He was too slow even to put his hands over his face and pull up his knees to protect himself. But his brain was alert enough to know that he was about to be impaled on the wood. He knew that he could not survive the blow.

In that split second of confusion, he felt something heavy land beside him, thudding painfully against his arm. The tree branch slammed down and crunched into metal rather than flesh and bone. Luke turned his head and felt warm blood on his neck. Next to him on the bed, his mobile had taken the full force of the fallen conifer's vicious branch.

Malc's flashing red light—his heartbeat—was extinguished.

When Luke fully came back to his senses, he was occupying the room next to Brooke Adams in Hounslow Medical Center. His first reaction was to look around for his constant companion, but there was no sign of Malc. A doctor was smiling at him. "Congratulations. You're alive. From what I hear, you shouldn't be. I've extracted all the pieces of glass. Thirty-two stitches in various cuts. You'll have aches and pains for a while and a couple of permanent battle scars. That's all. You can go once you've rested. For now, you've got a visitor."

"Malc?"

Still grinning, the doctor shook his head. "I don't think so. She's female for one thing. I'm told that she's a very important person around here. I'll leave you to it."

When he opened the door to go, Jade flew in. She strode up to Luke's bed and put out her arm to touch him but withdrew it before she made contact. "You really scared me, Luke!" she cried. "They tell me that you're lucky you survived. If it wasn't for Malc . . ."

"Where is he?"

"In for repairs. Like you. How are you?"

"Feeling battered. Unbelievable headache. But okay." He struggled to sit up.

"They've given you something for the pain. It'll kick in soon, the doctor said."

Luke put his hand gently on his cheek and felt a rough swelling.

"I don't think you're supposed to prod it."

Trying to smile, Luke said, "It hasn't ruined my good looks, has it?"

"Not entirely," she answered.

"Do you know what happened? It was the tree, wasn't it?"

Jade nodded. "Crashed through the roof and window, into your room."

He groaned. "I bet it didn't touch the official musician's room."

"Of course not. It wouldn't dare."

Luke laughed softly. Through the screaming in his head, though, he wondered if he was merely a victim of a storm or, like Brooke, a victim of Spoilsport. Had Hounslow notched up another mishap or another crime? "I don't know what I'm going to do without Malc."

"Nothing at all," Jade insisted. "You rest. You can rush around after crooks tomorrow."

Chapter Fourteen

On Monday morning, in a new room within Hounslow Residential, Luke looked in the mirror and groaned. The rip in his left cheek and the wound in his neck were still ugly and inflamed. His hands, arms, and the rest of his face were covered in dots, curls, and dashes of dried blood. And his skin was deep purple in places. When he moved, he shuffled like Frank Russell, as if he'd aged several years. Not even a pomegranate breakfast had cured his tenderness.

He stopped peering at himself and instead wandered all of the way around Malc. There wasn't even a dent in his metal jacket. "Weren't you damaged?" Luke asked.

"My exterior suffered severe mutilation and had to be replaced. Several of my facilities remain broken. I am running on a minimum forensic capability until further repairs can be effected, but my defensive capabilities have been overhauled and updated. Very few circuit boards were corrupted. These have been exchanged. However, I have lost all data on reptiles recorded in the third-floor corridor on Saturday evening."

Luke didn't mind, because the lizard count had simply been a tactic to divert Malc. "Are you still my Malc, though?"

"Confirmed."

"Tell me what a wild-goose chase is."

"According to a recent entry in my dictionary, it is a waste of time."

"No, it's not a waste of time, Malc. It's told me you really are you." Luke's wide grin caused an uncomfortable tension in the stitched wound on his cheek.

Malc paused, unable to compute Luke's meaning.

"Never mind. We've got a case to crack. That means, a crime to solve. But . . . er . . . first I have to say thanks."

"Gratitude is unnecessary."

"So you keep telling me, but . . . I'm alive thanks to you."

"I carried out my function successfully."

Luke smiled wryly. It seemed odd to him that his mobile would have been equally unaffected if he had died. There would have been no regret, merely a failure to complete a program, like a task aborted because of a computer error. And then Malc would have been assigned to a different FI. "Anyway, I'm feeling lucky now. And I might have a new crime scene right outside my window." He headed for the door and moaned at the effort. "Sore as well as lucky. I think I'll risk the elevator. I'm not in the mood for charging up and down steps."

The conifer was leaning against the apartment block with several branches embedded in the building. It had brought up with it a great big disk of mud encasing its exposed roots.

"The question is," Luke said, not going too close in case it was a crime scene, "what made it collapse? The weather? Did the rain make the ground unstable and the wind blow it

down, or did someone give it a little help? Was it a deliberate attempt to get rid of me?" He shivered at the thought.

Malc went forward and, hovering over the disturbed patch of ground, carried out a fine scan. Then he reported, "There are clear signs that the ground has been levered up by a tool such as a spade. The compacting of the soil shows that the implement was pushed deep into the ground and pulled back at least twenty-seven times on the side farthest away from the building. This had the effect of directing the subsequent fall toward the accommodation block, and your room specifically."

Trying not to think about the fact that the case had become personal, Luke said, "Record all shoeprints and any artifacts within fifteen feet that could belong to whoever did it."

"I have already logged those details as standard procedure."

"Any luck?"

"I do not experience random acts of fortune."

"That's my mobile," Luke muttered under his breath. Then he asked, "What have you found?"

"There are no clearly relevant traces. There are at least eleven impressions of different shoes. The prints interfere with one another, making analysis ambiguous. Also, rain has degraded some patterns. Most are typical of heavy work shoes. Two are characteristic of training shoes."

"This might've been done just to wreck the building,"

Luke said, "but if it was an attempt to kill me, Spoilsport must have set it up sometime between Thursday—when I arrived—and Saturday night's storm."

"That is logical and valid speculation."

Luke replied, "I'm going to interview Holly Queenan again. On the way, check with The Authorities to see if I'm allowed to offer her a computer in exchange for any information she might be holding back."

"Processing request."

The holding cell was plain and clean. The windowless room contained a bed, table, chair, toilet, sink, and shower. It certainly wasn't a palace, but for Holly, it was ten times better than sleeping rough.

From the bed where she was lounging, she looked up at her visitor in surprise. "What happened to you?" she said.

"Don't you know?" asked Luke.

"How could I? You locked me away in here." She twisted around to sit on the edge of the bed.

Carefully, Luke lowered himself onto the chair. "Where were you at about seven-forty-five on Monday morning?"

She shrugged without thinking.

Luke looked around the room. "You could put a computer on the table. That'd relieve the boredom. Of course, if you cooperated with me, I might be able to send you home—and you could take it with you."

She laughed caustically "I live out of a plastic bag. No

115

use to me without electricity."

"So why were you trying to steal one from the sports stadium?"

"To trade. It's a commodity."

"I can still get you one."

"What's the deal?"

"Where were you at seven-forty-five on Monday morning?" he repeated.

This time, she paused. "Monday. I was in the warm-up area next to the stadium."

Luke asked, "What were you doing there?"

"Warming up."

Luke cocked his head to one side and then wished that he hadn't when the movement stretched his neck wound. He flinched. "Fair enough, I suppose. What were you warming up for?"

Holly sighed with impatience. "You've never slept rough, have you? I sleep in and around the stadium. Sometimes in bulldozers. Anywhere, really. Anywhere dry. But not usually warm. I get up at first light—before the builders come—and run around to get warm."

"Would you recognize Libby Byrne?"

"You mentioned her before. Who is she?"

Luke pointed at the blank wall across from Holly. "Put up a picture, Malc." When the image appeared a few seconds later, Luke squinted at it and said to his mobile, "It's a little fuzzy."

"I am working at lower resolution than normal."

"Oh. Well, it's good enough." Turning to Holly again, he said, "Did you see her on Monday? She's the boss."

Holly shook her head.

"All right." Changing tack, he said, "Have you ever gone into the Aquatic Center?"

"Nothing worth taking in there."

"So you've been in there to find out."

"I looked in through the windows."

"Was there water in the pool the last time you looked?"

"No."

"If you hang out around the stadium, have you ever seen someone going up the ladders and messing around with the scaffolding?"

"Yes. Lots."

"Aside from builders," Luke said patiently. "I mean, anyone suspicious. Probably at an unusual time, like late at night or early in the morning."

Holly shook her head.

"What about the large tree outside Hounslow Residential. Do you know it?"

Holly's mood changed at once. She laughed. "I'll tell you one reason why it's still there. I stopped them from chopping it down by camping in it."

"Have you been near it since Thursday?"

"Yes."

"When was that?"

"Friday night."

"What were you doing?"

"Nothing," she answered. "Just thinking about past protests. I'm fond of that old evergreen."

"Did you see anything while you were there?"

"Yes."

Luke sat bolt upright. "What?"

"Lights on in some of the rooms, pigeons, a couple of workers leaving the building . . ."

It was the sort of deadpan response that Malc would have given. "Did you see anything suspicious?"

Stalling, she asked, "When do I get this computer?"

"Tomorrow, I would think. If I give the go-ahead."

"In that case, yes, I saw a woman. Around my age, I think."

"What was she doing?"

"I don't know. It was pretty dark, but she was scratching around in the dirt. When she saw me, she ran off."

"Was she carrying anything?"

"A big bag of some sort."

"Would you recognize her again?"

"Maybe."

"Was it Libby Byrne?" He jerked a thumb toward the wall where Malc had projected the low-quality picture.

"No. The one at the tree was younger."

"Okay." Talking to his mobile, Luke said, "Let's try

Venetia Murray, the nurse."

Holly watched the image appear and then nodded. "Yes. That's her."

"Certain?"

"Totally."

"Thanks. That's useful." He glanced down at her muddy shoes and asked, "Were you wearing those on Friday night?"

"Always."

"Lift them up, please, so my mobile can scan the tread."

"Why?"

"He has a lot of shoeprints from around the tree. I want to eliminate yours, if they're there."

She sighed but straightened her knees so that Malc could record both patterns.

"Thanks," said Luke. He stood up to leave.

"Don't forget your promise," Holly snapped, as if she didn't trust him.

"Malc, have I cleared it with The Authorities to give Holly Queenan a new computer?"

"Confirmed."

Knowing that she could rely on a Mobile Aid to Law and Crime to tell the truth, Holly nodded.

"Order it now," Luke said to Malc. "To arrive as soon as possible. And I want The Authorities to know that Holly's been helpful to my case. They should take it into account when they decide what to do about the charges against her. I'd support canceling them."

"Transmitting message."

Holly watched him limping to the door. "You look like I did when I fell out of the tree once." Then she smiled at him.

Chapter Fifteen

When Luke and Malc arrived at William Underwood's living quarters in Ealing, the nurse was preparing her patient's medicine. She looked at Luke's torn face, hesitated, but decided not to remark on it. Perhaps she was too polite, nervous, or distracted. "I have to . . . um . . ." She pointed to an internal door and said, "The poor old thing needs his medication."

"No problem," Luke replied. "Carry on." He followed her into the kitchen, where she had just mixed his drugs with the required volume of water.

Lifting up and examining a hypodermic syringe, she said, "Now that I've gotten this far, I should carry on." She bent down and filled the barrel with the solution.

Luke looked down at her shoes. They were perfectly clean.

Venetia held the syringe upright, tapped the barrel to dislodge any air, and then squirted a little of the liquid out into the air like a mini fountain until she had the right dose. "I'll just go and . . ." She nodded toward the bedroom.

While she was out of the kitchen, Malc spoke to Luke using his quietest setting. "I recorded a used barrel from a hypodermic syringe beside Hounslow cab terminus on Saturday afternoon. However, it is not admissible evidence

121

because its origin, ownership, and timescale are unknown."

"Was it the same type that she just used?"

"Yes."

"If we go back," Luke whispered, "could you analyze the inside to find out what was in it?"

"It is highly unlikely that any of its liquid content remains. Sunlight and physical weathering will have degraded it, and recent rainfall will have washed it away. In addition, chemical analysis would also be inadmissible for the same reason."

"How about fingerprints on it? That would go a long way toward solving the ownership problem."

Malc went silent for a few seconds and then replied, "My scan did not reveal fingerprints on the visible parts."

Venetia came back into the kitchen with an empty syringe and disposed of it.

"I'm sorry about this," Luke said to her, "but, when I saw you on Saturday, I forgot to ask you where were you between seven-thirty and eight last Monday morning."

"In a cab, on my way here. To see my Ealing patients."

"How about Friday night?"

"Friday night?" Venetia muttered, apparently to give herself time to think.

"That's right."

"I . . . um . . . stayed in. Nothing exciting, I'm afraid." She tried to smile and shrug casually, but she didn't succeed. She just looked uneasy.

"That's strange, because I have a witness who saw you up near Hounslow Residential."

Venetia frowned. "Really? Are you sure . . . ?"

"After this, I'm going to your home. Now that you're linked to my investigation through an eyewitness, I've got the authority to go into your apartment and scan all your shoes. Is that true, Malc?"

"Correct."

"Even if you've cleaned the pair that you were wearing on Friday," Luke continued, "Malc only needs a speck of mud to match with the soil outside of the accommodation block. No one's that good at cleaning undersoles. On top of that, no matter how clean or dirty they are, Malc will match their size and tread with the shoeprints that he found at the scene. Or maybe you're still wearing the same ones now. That would save me the trouble of going to your place. Either way, it won't take long to back up what the witness told me."

"What do you want to know?"

"What you were doing by the tree."

Luke watched Venetia peeling off her medical gloves and realized that there was a reason why fingerprints might never have appeared on the muddy syringe barrel by the cab tracks.

Venetia dropped the gloves into the garbage. Then she turned toward Luke but did not make eye contact. "You know what I was doing."

"Do I?"

"Yes."

"You were digging up its roots, for one thing."

Venetia frowned and then shook her head. "Not digging, no. Not really. I thought I saw a lizard—it could've been one of William's—and I was just trying to see where it had gone. There were quite a few holes by the tree. I thought that it might have gone down one."

"Are you sure? Didn't you make the holes?"

"No."

"What did you have in your bag? It was rather big. A spade, was it?"

"It wasn't that big. And there wasn't anything in it. If I found a lizard or snake, I'd have to put it somewhere to bring it back here."

"Mmm." Luke was not convinced by her explanation. "You're telling me that you were on another lizard hunt. That's not illegal. Weird, maybe, but not a crime. So, why did you start off saying that you stayed in on Friday night? Why lie to me if you have nothing to hide?"

"Because it's weird. I thought you might not believe me—or think I was up to no good."

"I'm surprised you went looking for something in the dark."

"Some of his reptiles are nocturnal."

"Why's it so important for you to please one of your patients?"

Venetia didn't have an answer. She shrugged helplessly. "He's . . . I don't know. It's such a shame, what the building's done to him, losing his wife and his pets. So sad. He's . . . affected me, I guess."

Malc soon provided Luke with some firm physical evidence. He identified a pair of brown boots that Venetia was wearing when she went up to the conifer. Of course, it wasn't evidence that Venetia Murray was Spoilsport. It only proved that she was near the scene of an attempted murder.

Back in Hounslow, Luke squatted beside the cab track and winced as he pulled tight latex gloves over the cuts and bruises on his hands. Then he dug his fingers carefully into the damp earth and pulled up the syringe barrel. It was heavier than he expected because it was filled with mud, but it came away with a sucking noise. Luke placed it inside of an evidence bag and pointed to the small dent that it had left in the dirt. "Can you sit on this and scoop up some soil?"

"Confirmed. What is the purpose of the sample?"

"I want you to analyze it for any drugs that might've leaked out into the dirt."

"That is irrelevant as I cannot enter any result into case notes."

"Yes, but I still want you to do it. I'm short on forensic evidence so I've got to squeeze everything I can out

of things like this."

"Assuming that the quantity of any such substance is at trace level, my current resources are not sufficient to perform a spectroscopic identification. I would have to arrange for the material to be analyzed in a fully equipped chemical laboratory."

"Fair enough. Take the sample and let's get going. I'm aching in places I didn't know I had. I need to sit still for a while and recharge my batteries."

"You do not . . ."

Luke put up his hand. "I need a rest."

Arriving at Hounslow Residential, Luke paid the manager a quick visit before going up to his new quarters. Luke knew that anyone with a bit of initiative could have found out which room was his. It wasn't a closely guarded secret, and the information could have leaked from any of the staff, the bookings list, or the computer. Even so, he thought that it was worth checking if Spoilsport had been nosing around before the tree uprooted. "Has anyone shown an interest in my room number since I arrived?" he asked.

"Yes," the manager replied right away.

The answer took Luke by surprise, and his heart rate leaped. "Oh? Who was that?"

"The Games' musician. Ms. Vernon. I hope you don't mind that I told her your room number. She said that you were friends and she wanted to surprise you."

Luke smiled and nodded. "That's fine. It was a nice surprise. Anyone else?"

"Not that I'm aware of."

On the way up the stairs, Malc said, "Even though Jade Vernon made this inquiry into your room number, she should not be considered as a strong suspect because of her location. At the time of the majority of the sabotage incidents, she was in Birmingham or Sheffield."

"Thanks, Malc," Luke replied, his tone dripping with irony that his mobile would not understand. "That's helpful. I'll rule out my best friend from trying to kill me."

Sitting at the table in his new quarters, Luke was aware that the syringe might have nothing whatsoever to do with his case. An athlete using bodybuilding drugs might have cast it aside carelessly. A doctor or nurse might have dropped it accidentally. But Luke was intrigued because Malc had found it at the cab terminus where Spoilsport may have abducted Libby Byrne. Perhaps the saboteur had injected her with a drug but there'd been a scuffle before the contents of the syringe had taken effect. Perhaps the barrel had spilled unnoticed from Spoilsport's hand in the struggle.

Luke took the plastic barrel between his gloved finger and thumb. He dipped it into a bowl of warm water and moved it gently back and forth to clean off the mud. After a few minutes, the soil had sunk to the bottom of the

bowl, and he was holding a cleansed syringe barrel.

He shook the water off his red herring or vital clue and held it up by the narrow end for Malc to scan. "Any prints now?" he asked eagerly.

"No."

He balanced it on a tissue and said, "Try your best enhancements."

"I only have one working enhancement. I can reconstruct any invisible impressions by exposing the object to the fumes of cyanoacrylate superglue and then viewing it in infrared radiation. Components or the superglue will adhere to the fatty acids, amino acids, protein, and urea in human fingerprints, and these are highly distinguishable in the infrared part of the spectrum."

"Yeah. All right." Luke's head was aching. He just wanted a result. "I'm going to lie down while you do it. Then there's this bowl of water, the grunge at the bottom, and the dirt sample that you took. I need chemical analyses on them all, looking for a drug that might've been in the syringe."

"Tasks logged."

Luke took two of the painkillers that he'd been given and headed for the bedroom.

Chapter Sixteen

Luke only snatched a few minutes of rest before a security guard escorted a bedraggled protester to his door. With his hands on his hips, Luke smiled wryly as he watched Frank Russell hobbling into the apartment. "I asked to see you when you got into your next bit of mischief. What have you done this time?"

Wet and windswept, Frank stood in the middle of the room and swayed slightly from side to side. "Not a lot, compared with ruining what's left of my life. They caught me injecting glue into a few locks, that's all."

Luke shook his head. "When I saw you on the runway, you made a comment about how young I was." He picked up a glass vase from the desk. "Because I was the youngest-ever FI when I graduated from Birmingham, they gave me this." Pretending that the fragile vase was an award, he clutched it proudly to his chest. "It's very important to me." Without warning, he flung it in Frank's direction, a couple of feet to his right.

Acting on instinct, all signs of the sluggish old man evaporated. Frank stepped sideways and caught the vase deftly in both hands.

Luke gazed at him for a second, letting the implication sink in. "You've been pretending, haven't you, Frank?

You're not as sick as you've led me to believe."

Frank stared at the vase safely cushioned in his cupped hands like a well-caught rugby ball and realized that he'd been found out. "You won't tell anyone else, will you?" he said.

"Why do you act like you're on your last legs, faking lung cancer?"

Sighing, Frank sat down and placed the glass vase on his lap. "You are young. At your age, you don't think about what it's like to be old. It isn't pretty. So, I exaggerate a little. That way, people have more sympathy, and my protests get more attention."

"It hasn't really worked, though," Luke replied. "Maybe it's having the opposite effect. Maybe the builders think that they can ignore you because you won't be protesting much longer."

Frank's head drooped. "I hadn't thought of that."

"So, how healthy are you? If you had to go up a ladder, could you do it?"

"A stepladder's more my thing. I'm not good on big ladders. I get shaky."

"What about digging? You're an expert digger, aren't you? That's what you did in your garden."

"Used to," Frank stressed. "These days, it does my back in."

"Where were you last Monday morning, around quarter to eight?"

Frank shrugged. "Not a clue. I might be a bit better than

I pretend, but there's not much that I can do about a worn-out brain. I don't remember day-to-day things." He laughed dryly. "I can tell you everything I did when I was a boy, everything about my pigeons, but nothing about a few days ago. Hopeless. It's age, you know. The brain goes, the waterworks get bad, bones ache, and the spine . . . I told you, it isn't pretty."

Luke had no real way of knowing if Frank was trying to pull the wool over his eyes again. If he was, Luke could find out only by getting physical evidence that incriminated him. "By the look of your shoes, you've been walking in mud. Lift them up for me, please. I want Malc to scan them."

Without question, Frank leaned back and lifted his legs one at a time. "I haven't been anywhere near the tree, if that's what's on your mind."

At once, Luke asked, "What makes you think that I'm interested in a tree?"

"I heard what happened and saw it myself when I went past today. Now you're asking about digging, shoes, and soil. And you look like you picked an argument with a tree." He chuckled. "I think you lost."

"Your brain seems pretty sharp to me."

"There's something else I heard. There's a musician checking things out."

"Oh?"

"Word gets around."

"What are you trying to say?" Luke asked.

"You ought to look out for her. She's part of the Games now, isn't she? She could be a target for an objector. She needs to be careful."

"Is that a threat?"

"Me? No. I'm trying to help. My campaign's peaceful, like I told you. But I'm not the only one, am I? There's a nastier piece of work than me out there."

"What have you heard? Who is it?"

Frank shrugged. "Nothing on the breeze about that. Sorry."

Luke didn't want to prolong the interview. "All right, Frank. That's enough. The guard'll be waiting for you outside. She'll probably take you somewhere where you can't do any harm—until she turns her back."

Frank got onto his feet, and the vase on his lap tumbled to the bare wood floor, where it broke into three large pieces.

Frank looked down and muttered, "There I go again. Forgetting it was there. Hopeless."

"It doesn't matter," Luke said. "Anyway, I hear that you're good with glue. You could put it back together again."

Frank let out a little laugh, believing that he'd made a friend.

"By the way," Luke added, "what were you using to squirt the glue?"

"A what-do-you-call-it. A plastic syringe thing."

Luke nodded. "I'll see you next time." As soon as the door closed behind Frank, Luke asked Malc, "What's the latest? Did you get any fingerprints off that syringe barrel?"

"No."

Luke pointed to the broken vase and said, "For the record, take Frank's prints off the glass."

"Scanning."

"And what about chemical analysis of the mud?"

"Any biologically active compounds are below my current detection limits. An agent will collect the samples later today and take them for further examination in The Authorities' forensic laboratory. However, the result will not be valid unless you can provide an unambiguous link to a suspect or a victim."

Luke's next visitor was Jade. This time, she hadn't brought a trolley laden with food and drinks. Still feeling unnerved and tense after his interview with Frank Russell, Luke looked at her and said, "I was wondering. Can you do the rest of your work in Sheffield?"

"What's this?" Jade exclaimed. "Are you trying to get rid of me?"

"No, of course not."

"You are, FI Harding! There's something going on. I can tell."

"I want you here. Obviously. But . . ."

"What?"

Luke swallowed. "Well, you know the Games are in danger. You've become part of it."

Jade waved her hand dismissively. "My part has nothing to do with the building. I won't make the difference between whether the Games go ahead or not. I'm not important like that. You could have the sports without the opening ceremony and anthem."

"One of my suspects has just vaguely threatened you."

Jade shook her head impatiently. "You're in Spoilsport's sights more than me." She nodded toward the gash on his left cheek. "That's more than a vague threat."

"I have Malc. You don't."

Jade sighed. "As it happens," she said, "I came to tell you that I've done everything I can here. I'm leaving in the morning. Back to the sunny North to work on the composition. I thought that you'd be disappointed, not eager to see me go."

Luke felt torn. "I *am* disappointed. You know I am. But at least you'll be safe in Sheffield."

Jade turned toward Malc and said, "He's useless at staying out of harm's way, so make sure that he's okay." Talking to Luke again, she added, "And don't you mess up, either. I want you alive to make sure that these games aren't canceled. Remember, it's the future of my career you're looking out for." Then she gave one of her irresistible smiles to show that she wasn't serious.

Chapter Seventeen

Neil Gladwin put down his coffee mug. His expression transformed from harassed site manager to concerned colleague as soon as he peered into Luke's flawed face. "I am sorry . . . Are you all right?"

"I've been better," Luke replied, "but I'm still in action." Then he added, "Someone won't be happy about that."

"What? Do you think that it was deliberate?"

"I know that it was. The aim was to trash either the building or me."

Neil shook his head in disgust. "Well, I've taken a team off other duties to remove the tree and repair the building, starting today. I could have done without the distraction, to be honest. It should have been cut down ages ago, but there was a problem with campaigners. One of them even began staying in its branches to stop it from being cut down."

"That was the woman you saw me arresting on Saturday morning."

"I thought that she looked familiar."

"Mmm." Changing the subject, Luke said, "Do you remember a couple of years ago, Libby was going on a trip to Glasgow?"

"Yes?" His response sounded more like a question than

an answer. It seemed that he wasn't going to admit that he could recall the aborted journey until he knew where Luke's interview was leading.

"Why didn't she take it?"

"Just as well that she didn't. It crashed."

"Yeah. But why didn't she go?"

"I can't remember the exact reason. It was a long time ago. Something cropped up here, I think."

"Something unexpected?"

Neil shrugged. "I guess it must have been. She wouldn't have planned to miss the plane, would she?"

"It must have been something that you couldn't handle in her absence."

Smirking, Neil replied, "No. It was something that *she thought* I couldn't handle in her absence. Big difference. I suspect that I could've sorted it out in no time."

"Have you been near that conifer in the last few days?"

"I've been past it—if that's any use to you—but not near it in the sense of touching the thing."

"To eliminate your shoeprints, I want Malc to scan yours." Luke looked at the pairs of sturdy shoes lined up on the floor under the overalls and hard hats.

"Fine. I use the ones on the right. The smaller ones on the left are Libby's. I haven't put them away."

Gritting his teeth, Luke knelt down. He slipped into his gloves and turned all of the toe-capped shoes upside down, exposing their undersoles. Then Malc moved closer to complete a scan.

"Whose are the others?" Luke asked.

Neil shrugged. "Spares, really. For me or a visitor or anyone."

"I guess you knew which room I was staying in."

Neil stared at him for a moment before saying, "Well, I could've found out easily enough, if I'd wanted to." He pointed to his computer. "I can log on and get the rooms where my workers are staying—so I can contact them in a hurry if I have to—so you're probably listed as well."

Malc said, "There is an eighty-seven percent match between the tread, size, and wear pattern of the shoes on the right and the impressions left within four point six feet of the conifer. Certainty is not possible because the recorded impressions are smudged and weathered. However, they are the most commonly occurring shoeprints beside the tree, and they coincide with the position of the spade marks."

Luke gazed at Neil Gladwin without a word. He waited for the uneasy silence to force him into speaking.

"But . . ." Neil spluttered. "It wasn't me. I don't know how . . ." He switched his gaze from Luke to Malc and back again. "It's crazy. Why would I mess up the schedule that I'm doing my best to stick to? I'm not going to build with one hand and pull down with the other, am I?" He nodded toward Malc. "And your robot said that it couldn't be certain."

"Eighty-seven percent," Luke replied. "That's a lot." He hesitated, doing a quick calculation in his head. "If you'd done eighty-seven percent of the three-thousand meters, you'd be on the final lap."

Neil spread his arms in a gesture of innocence. "The shoes are always here—so I can slip into them when I have to go out on site. Anyone could've come in and used them."

"Is the door unlocked all the time?"

The site manager grasped the chance to accuse someone else. "Yes. Except overnight, of course."

"Have they ever disappeared?"

Neil broke eye contact. He seemed to want to tell a lie but realized that his hesitation would give him away. "I can't say that I've noticed, to be honest."

"Have they ever been moved or gotten an extra layer of mud?"

"I'm a busy man. I don't exactly keep them under surveillance, but, yes, they might have been moved. Now that you mention it, I thought that there was something a bit different about them on Friday."

Luke ignored the comment. It was coming from a man who was desperate to show that he wasn't guilty. Luke pulled two large evidence bags out of his pocket and turned the work shoes over again. "I'm going to take them with me but, for now, do a fine scan on as much of the insides as you can, Malc. I'm looking for fibers from socks. Flakes of skin would be even better."

Luke felt relieved. At last, he was doing the job that he loved. Instead of talking to one suspect after another, he was using forensic methods to narrow down the options. With real evidence came real progress. Talking to Neil again, he said, "I'm going to your home to take a few fibers from every pair of socks you own. That way, I can see if there are any inside of the boots that don't belong to you. While I'm here, I'll get some from the socks that you're wearing. Put your feet up, please." Luke took a piece of tape and pressed it briefly against Neil's socks. When he tore it away, the tape had a lot of colored threads adhering to it. "By the way," Luke said as he put the captured fibers into a bag and sealed it, "you won't get the boots back. I'll destroy them to get every last trace out of the inside."

Neil shrugged. "Anything to prove that someone else has put them on."

"And I need your DNA to check against any skin. Do you want to yank a hair out—with its root—or shall I get Malc to sample a bit of saliva from the rim of your mug? He'll record your fingerprints while he's at it."

It was likely that the building manager's shoes had trampled all over the soil by the conifer and that was enough for Luke to move Neil Gladwin ahead of Venetia Murray, Libby Byrne, and Frank Russell on the list of

suspects in his head. The site manager's motive might be obscure, but maybe he was still upset that he was only a substitute. Besides, Malc had not discovered a match between Libby's or Frank's shoes and the impressions outside of Hounslow Residential. Luke wanted to interview Trevor Twigg again, and he was eager to talk to Owen and Jed, but the prospect of coaxing physical clues from Gladwin's hefty shoes was too enticing to delay.

The ten-inch shoes—almost boots—were medium size for a man or large for a woman. Luke placed them on a clean plastic sheet, and Malc subjected them to the most thorough tests that were still available to him. Once the mobile had explored the accessible outer parts, he split them open from the tongue to the toe with his laser. Luke peeled back the tough, synthetic material, allowing Malc to scan all of the insides.

"The only fingerprints on the outer surface belong to Neil Gladwin," Malc reported. "The combination of microscopic quartz grains in the soil adhering to the undersole is identical to that outside of Hounslow Residential. This result increases the probability that these shoes were responsible for the impressions near the conifer. I cannot calculate the current degree of confidence without testing more footwear and soil samples from different locations around the building site, but it is more than ninety percent. There is no other valid information from the exterior of the shoes."

"What about the insides?" Luke asked eagerly.

"There are fine particles of the same soil, along with common leaf fragments. There are no traces of human skin. There is a total of fourteen different fibers. The site manager's socks sampled today can account for thirteen. The remaining type of thread occurs in both boots. It is a regular sky-blue wool."

"Interesting."

"Near both toe caps, I detect an unknown white powder. Analysis in progress."

"Anything else?"

"No."

"All right. See if you can get me a visual connection to Trevor Twigg while you work on that white powder."

The historian's lined face covered the wall across from Luke. He didn't seem surprised or concerned at all by the wounds on Luke's head and shoulders appearing on his own telescreen. "What can I do for you?" he said coldly.

Luke decided to try shock tactics. "It's a bit of a coincidence that I bothered you on Saturday, and a few hours later someone tried to put me out of action."

"Did they? What do you mean?"

Luke's fingers lingered near the stitched wound on his cheek.

"Oh. I see," Trevor said.

Most people would have asked how he'd been hurt,

whether he was getting better, or even if they were under suspicion. The historian wasn't concerned. Luke had learned from their previous meeting that Trevor did not seem to care about anyone or anything aside from history, himself, and fishing. But right now, that didn't make him guilty of anything except self-interest. "Where were you on Saturday night?"

"I was at home with my partner, enjoying fresh mackerel."

"You caught cod."

"Yes. But after you left, I had a run on mackerel. A school came through, and they're stupid. They snap at anything shiny. I didn't have a spinner, so I caught them on a bait of tinfoil, believe it or not. You can yank them out two or three at a time."

"Your partner will confirm this?"

"Of course."

Luke nodded. He had no intention of talking to Trevor's partner, because her testimony would be unreliable and inadmissible. She would back up Trevor Twigg's story either because it was true or because she was protecting him. The alibi would be worthless. "What's your shoe size?" he asked.

"Nine and a half inches."

Again reserving his talkativeness for fishing and his curiosity for history, Twigg didn't ask why Luke wanted to know. But Luke noted that he could have worn Neil

Gladwin's shoes comfortably because they were one size larger than his own. "Do you know where the site manager's office is?"

Trevor laughed with contempt. "I went often enough to complain."

"Right, well, I'm stuck here in the London area for the moment so I'm sending an agent out to see you."

Trevor shrugged.

"I need a few samples—nothing serious—to help my inquiries." Luke was not going to let on that he was interested in sky-blue socks. If he had, Trevor would surely have disposed of them before the agent arrived.

"Fine," Trevor replied tersely. "You're an FI. I can't stop you."

Luke's job would have been a lot easier if there was a rule that the innocent were friendly and the guilty unpleasant. In his short career, he'd already met friendly criminals and unpleasant people who were perfectly innocent, yet unhelpful. Luke was still making up his mind about Trevor Twigg.

Chapter Eighteen

Once again, Luke was on a river launch, heading for the dome in Greenwich. And again, a cold wind was channeling down the Thames river. The speed of the boat made it seem stronger than it really was. Luke had to brush hair away from his eyes every few minutes.

Indifferent to the wind, Malc perched on the deck and said, "I have completed the analysis of the white dust in both work shoes belonging to the new site manager. It is zinc oxide and chlorphenesin."

"What's that?"

"It is a powder used as an antifungal agent for treating ringworm, commonly called athlete's foot. The dust is applied liberally to the toes and the insides of socks to treat the infection. It is inevitable that some of the fine powder penetrates the weave of the material and settles in the shoes of a person undergoing treatment."

"So," Luke said loudly over the wailing wind, "I'm looking for someone with a shoe size of ten inches or less, sky-blue woolen socks, and athlete's foot." He paused before adding, "There are plenty of athletes around Hounslow, so there'll be plenty of athlete's foot."

Not recognizing the humor in Luke's words, Malc replied, "The name of the condition is misleading. It is not restricted to athletes. The fungus is highly infectious, and it can spread in areas where people often go barefoot, including sports changing rooms and the edges of swimming pools. That is the only known association with athletes and the reason for its name." Luke's mobile added, "You should check on the clinical status of Neil Gladwin's feet."

"I wish I'd thought of that," Luke replied sarcastically. With a smile, he said, "*You* should check his medical records. And all the suspects' files."

Malc's reaction was as factual and efficient as ever. "Task logged. However, the condition is not usually serious enough to warrant medical intervention."

"So people treat themselves with this antifungal powder."

"Correct."

"Pity," Luke remarked. "Search medical files anyway. Just in case." He paused and then asked, "Did you detect the same powder around the edge of the swimming pool in the Aquatic Center?"

"No."

As soon as Luke entered the huge sports dome, Owen called out, "Hey! Who's been using you as an archery target?" He laughed loudly.

"Very funny," Luke replied, also unable to suppress a grin. In a way, he liked having wounds, now that the pain had subsided. They were a visible testament to the danger of his job. He could wear them proudly, like an athlete's team colors.

Once Jed had stopped shouting instructions at two of the runners on the indoor track, he jogged up to Luke and Owen.

"I came to ask you about bodybuilding drugs," said Luke. "Do athletes still inject them?"

It was Jed who answered. "Not these days. Not unless they're really stupid. Anabolics are too easy to detect with LAPPED. It's all a lot more subtle now."

"What do you mean?"

"If someone's going to cheat, they'll take growth hormone."

"Growth hormone?"

Jed nodded. "Nature puts it in the body anyway, so finding it isn't enough to prove that someone's not playing fair. LAPPED looks for athletes who've got five to ten times the normal level and then disqualifies them. What it does is make new muscle cells. Lots of them."

"Who supplies it?"

"Ah. Now, that's the interesting thing." Jed's expression was half grimace, half grin. "They find shady pathologists who'll extract GH from dead bodies."

"Yuck. Really?"

Owen's expression was all smiles. "Likely, some athletes are so keen to win, they get GH from vets and inject that."

"Not dead vets," Jed joked. "Mainly from slaughtered

pigs. It's a silly idea because it doesn't do anything. I don't know why. It's something biological—animal and human cells work differently."

"Are there any side effects?"

"It's dangerous," Owen answered.

Jed filled in the details. "The muscles bulk up all right, but so do the organs. Your heart can fail. A few have died. Before it gets to that stage, you can see overgrown jaws, hands, and feet."

"Is that what Ford Drayton's been up to?"

Jed shook his head. "It's not like he has supernatural strength or anything. He's strong enough to run at a good pace for two hours, and that's it. Nothing out of the ordinary there. It's down to his technique, I'm sure."

"Good coaching, then."

"I don't remember Yvonne Chaplow being that good," Jed replied.

"What do you know about her?"

"Not a lot. Average coach. Very good on muscle movement, but she handles too many disciplines. Never concentrated on one thing enough to develop really special athletes."

"Until now," Luke remarked.

"I guess it means that she's stumbled across something."

"When I saw her," Luke told them, "she was desperate to keep what she was doing under wraps."

"Two possibilities, then," Jed replied. "It's legal but too good to share, or it's cheating."

Luke smiled and nodded. "Thanks. I'll try my luck with her again."

The Gymnastics Hall within the indoor arena was not yet ready for use but it was almost complete. Yvonne Chaplow and her most promising young gymnast—Saskia Frame—were examining the facilities, checking out the positions of the asymmetric bars, the balance beam, the vault, and the area for floor exercises. This time, the coach showed no sign of annoyance when Luke interrupted them.

"I don't suppose this," he said, waving an arm toward the performance area, "matches up to places in the North."

Yvonne hesitated, probably wondering why a forensic investigator would make such a comment, before answering. "Now that you mention it . . ."

To push her, Luke said, "I think that this regeneration thing is really good."

"It's got its merit. Agreed. It's great for Hounslow, I guess. But why rely on it for an important international tournament? I mean, is it going to be ready on time? Will it cope with the visitors? We've got fantastic venues in Newcastle, Manchester, and plenty of others. The gymnastics facilities in Bradford are the best in the world." She shrugged to show that she was astonished by the decision to stage the events in the South. "Regenerate Hounslow by all means, but consolidate the venue first."

Saskia Frame was tiny and as light as a feather. Luke knew that she was 14 years old, but she looked around 12 or 13 at the most. Her body was still growing, still incredibly flexible. She had draped a fluffy light-blue scarf around her neck and over one shoulder. It reminded Luke that Yvonne Chaplow's team color was sky blue. Looking down, he was surprised to note that the young gymnast's feet were out of proportion. They were almost as large as her coach's. Smiling at her, he said, "I bet athlete's foot is an occupational hazard for you."

"Sorry?" the girl replied, puzzled by his turn of phrase.

"Do you get athlete's foot?"

Yvonne interrupted. "Is this an official line of inquiry?"

"I'm just curious."

"It's not a big issue. If any of my competitors get it, I stop it from spreading around right away. There's a very effective powder."

"Does anyone have it at the moment?"

Yvonne eyed him suspiciously. With her hair held tightly back, she looked severe. "I don't think so."

"I guess you all have light-blue socks."

"Why do you ask?"

Luke shrugged. "It's your team color."

"Actually, our socks are traditional white."

Sensing that he wasn't going to get any more out of her

by pursuing that line of inquiry, he changed his tactics. "What's your attitude to performance-enhancing drugs?"

Yvonne gave herself a moment to think by adjusting her position against the vault. "Look, my kids don't use them. Never. It's against the rules. But it's no secret that I'd like to see the regulations changed."

"Oh?" Luke prompted.

"They don't make sense to me. Top athletes use the best running shoes, the best equipment, the best training regime, the best nutrition. Food's loaded with chemicals that make the body grow. That's why everyone eats. I can't see why performers shouldn't use the best drugs as well. It's just a step up from bodybuilding food. In fact, it's incredibly hard to tell the difference between a food and a drug at times. Food supplements fall halfway between the two. There wouldn't be the same confusion if drugs were legalized."

Luke frowned. "A lot of them can harm, though, can't they? Sports are supposed to be a celebration of what the body can do, not an excuse to damage it."

"I'll give you that," the trainer said. "I meant, legalize the ones that don't do any damage. Short term or long term."

"Is that Ford Drayton's secret?"

Offended, Yvonne stared at him. "I told you. My athletes don't do drugs. I don't agree with the rules, but I don't break them."

"Some people are saying . . ."

She interrupted. "They're wrong. He's clean. Always has been. LAPPED has shown that."

"What's his secret, then? You didn't want me to see when I gate-crashed your training session on Friday—by accident."

Yvonne's mood darkened even more. "I'm asking again. Are you investigating us?"

"In a way. And it's against the law not to answer my questions."

Saskia wandered around the vault and then strolled over to check out the asymmetric bars. She sneezed twice, and the noise seemed much too loud for the size of the girl.

Yvonne took a deep breath, apparently trying to stay calm. "Okay. It's all fair and aboveboard. It's all about his running shoes. They're a new type."

"Go on."

"We got a machine to make an exact model of his feet by scanning them with a laser. It's all digital. Then we got him to walk, run, and exercise on a special insole called a pedar. It records all of the forces acting on every part of the feet. With all that data, a computer can figure out the perfect design of shoe to fit his running style and protect his feet from injuries." She shrugged. "That's it. Not against the rules and not a drug in sight."

"Mmm. Tailor-made running shoes. How are they made?"

"That's high-tech as well. A computer sort of prints them out. I'm not the expert, but a laser beam blasts away at nylon particles and fuses them together. That way, it builds up the precise shape layer by layer. It's like printing, but in three dimensions. You end up with a flawless, lightweight shoe."

Luke nodded. He was surprised at Yvonne Chaplow's transformation from a quarrelsome and cagey coach to a talkative trainer. It was as if she'd decided to let him in on one advance to hide something else. "Interesting," he said. "Is that all?"

Yvonne opened up her palms and lifted her shoulders in a gesture of innocence. "Yes. That's my big secret."

"Thanks," Luke replied. Out of the corner of his eye, though, he spotted Saskia returning to her coach's side with reddening cheeks.

Chapter Nineteen

On his way out of the indoor arena, Luke heard three dull thuds coming from one of the game rooms. He halted in the passageway and listened. In the silence, he could make out the clear sound of footsteps. After a brief pause, there was another thud. Curious, Luke pushed the door open and looked inside.

Ian Pritchard—the rat catcher and vet—threw two more darts at the board and then, sensing someone behind him, turned around. "Ah," he said, clearly embarrassed. "Caught red-handed. I'm checking the poison and collecting dead rats, but I couldn't resist a sneaky game, could I? I love it, even playing solo."

With a big grin, Luke wandered into the room. "Looks like you need a bit of competition."

"You play, do you?"

Selecting a set of darts from the stand, Luke said, "I did. Before I took up chasing crooks."

Ian still seemed compelled to make an excuse for taking a break. He pointed toward his duffel bag in the corner. "I want you to know that I bagged up all of the rats before I started playing."

"As long as you didn't try picking them off with darts. But I'd be impressed if you could." Luke stepped up to the oche and made himself comfortable, fixing the triple 20 with his eye. His first dart didn't hit it, but it went very close. The next two darts followed the first, ending up in a tight line just under the wire.

"Nice grouping," Ian commented.

"Two more warm-up throws, then closest to the middle for five-zero-one?"

"Yeah. Okay." Ian hesitated before adding, "You've had a good doctor working on your cheek. Nice repair. What happened?"

Luke was more interested in the game than in talking through his scars yet again. Settling in and finding the target, he scored 85. "Just a cut or two when a tree fell on Hounslow Residential." Then he focused on double 16. Missed it twice and hit it once.

Ian watched Luke's throw closely and said, "Now you're scaring me." He looked around, searching for something. "How are we going to keep score? No computer."

"Yes, there is," Luke replied. "Do you know darts, Malc?"

"It is an indoor game with its origins in archery. Small arrowlike shafts are thrown at a segmented circular board, and points are scored according to where they land on the target. There are . . ."

"All right. You've convinced us. You're referee and scorekeeper."

The game took Luke back to his school days when he'd run onto a field and head a soccer ball, take a kick, catch a ball, and instantly became part of a game. Now that he was an FI, he missed that spontaneous fun. This crazy game of darts was the closest he came to making up for it. But it wasn't as carefree as it looked. After he won the first game on double eight, he said to Ian, "Have any athletes ever asked you to extract growth hormone from dead animals? Another game, by the way?"

"Sure. I want to even out the scores." Ian took his throw and muttered, "Sixty." Then, before his opponent settled himself at the oche, he added, "Growth hormone? Yes. It was a while ago. I remember someone—a man—asking me if I could get some from a dead pig."

Luke scored 100. "What did you do about it?"

"Nothing. Well, I didn't have a dead pig for one thing. Second, I didn't know why anyone would want growth hormone from a pig. Maybe a farmer trying to fatten up his stock." After his throw, he thrust a fist into the air, "One hundred and twenty-one."

"Good shot." Luke steadied himself. His body remained absolutely still. Only his right arm from the elbow to his fingertips moved when he threw a dart. The control over each flight came from the flick of his wrist.

Malc announced, "One hundred and forty."

"Did you realize what was going on?" Luke asked.

"Eventually. He wasn't a farmer. A weight lifter, I think. He was into power sports, anyway. I didn't think a hormone from a pig—or anywhere else—would do him

155

any good. For one thing, it could contain animal viruses, couldn't it? So I said no. That's the last I heard of it." He took his turn and scored 45.

"Sorry," said Luke. "That's me putting you off." He glanced again at Ian's duffel bag. It was zipped up so he couldn't see any plastic bags with their gruesome remains. "Just one more thing. What do you do with dead animals? Like the rats."

Ian smiled. "You might not believe it, but I do pretty much what we do with dead people. I have a crematorium. A pet crematorium and a garden to scatter or bury the ashes."

"Oh. I never knew that," Luke replied as he lined up his next throw.

"One hundred," Malc stated. "One hundred and sixty-one remaining."

"Are you sure that your mobile's not directing your darts?" Ian muttered with a pained grin.

"People tell me I'm good at aiming things, that's all."

"You're young. You should be playing in these youth games coming up in the spring, shouldn't you?"

"If only I had the time to put in the training," said Luke. "But I don't."

"Training! I wouldn't want to play you once you're trained up. You're relentless already!"

Luke won three to zero, thanked Ian for the game, and left in a good mood.

Part of the Hounslow plan was an innovative scheme for carrying aircraft passengers the short distance from the airport to the center of the development. The builders were making a covered moving walkway, like a conveyor belt for people and their luggage. Luke found Neil Gladwin near the stadium, talking to a supervisor about laying the foundations for the station at the end of the autocarrier. Next to them, a bulldozer idled until they'd made the necessary decisions.

Spotting Luke, Neil said to the supervisor, "Excuse me a second." Turning toward the FI, he asked anxiously, "Any news?"

Luke pulled him to one side, out of the hearing of the waiting workforce. "I just wondered if you've got athlete's foot."

The site manager looked puzzled. "What?"

"Have you got athlete's foot?"

"What is it? Something you get by running too much? You won't find me pounding the track!"

Malc had already informed Luke that none of the suspects' medical records mentioned the minor infection so Luke was going to have to check them one by one. "No," he explained. "It's a fungus. Not a big deal. It makes the toes itchy and blistered." As soon as he said it, Luke's mind went back to something that he'd noticed last Thursday, but he tried not to let it distract him now.

Neil shook his head. "Not something that I've come across."

Knowing that Neil could be lying, Luke said, "Are you sure? Remember, I can ask you to take your shoes and socks off and take a look right now."

Neil shrugged. "Feel free. I don't have anything to hide."

"You're in luck, then," Luke told him and walked away.

Neil called after him, "What was that about?"

Over his shoulder, Luke said, "I'll let you know."

If Gladwin was telling the truth, it meant that someone else had used his work shoes, just as he'd claimed. But that didn't prove that the manager was innocent. It only told Luke that there was another suspect: an unknown person with itchy feet.

It was standard practice for a forensic investigator to hide conclusions from suspects unless there was a very good reason to open up. As Luke strode toward the Hounslow cab terminus, he said to Malc, "I want to keep Neil in the dark."

Luke's mobile replied, "That would be classified as torture."

In exasperation, Luke closed his eyes for a moment and took a deep breath.

"As an FI supported by my analyses," Malc said, "you are qualified to look for traces of antifungal treatments. You are not qualified to identify a medical condition by examining suspects' feet. Only a doctor's diagnosis would be admissible in law."

"It's not like brain surgery, is it?"

"No. You are not qualified for either."

Luke laughed. "Let's just concentrate on the case. Sounds like I have to ask for a medical examination of all suspects' feet."

"I would support such a request to The Authorities."

"Okay. Go ahead. Let loose the podiatrists."

"Transmitting request."

"I want them to check out Brooke Adams as well."

"Confirmed. However, she is a victim, not a suspect."

Luke nodded. He knew that the swimmer made an improbable suspect because she'd taken a terrible punishment at the hands of Spoilsport, but her injuries might have been intended to divert the suspicions of an investigator. "If you replay Thursday's interview with her, you'll see that she rubbed her toes a lot."

"Exposure to toxic chemicals causes irritation," Malc told him.

"I know, but even so . . . Maybe she knew what she was diving into and went in just for a few seconds to hurt herself enough to put me off."

Malc replied, "She has no known motive, and her accident happened before your arrival. Therefore she cannot be responsible for the attempt on your life."

"Maybe she made the conifer unstable earlier. Maybe it was an attack on the building. Hitting my room—my first one—might have been sheer fluke."

"Speculation."

"I know that it's unlikely," Luke said. "So are asteroids hitting the planet, but they do. And there's something else. When the agent takes Trevor Twigg's sock samples to the lab, get them to check for the antifungal powder as well."

"Transmitting."

"I don't suppose I have a result from that soil by the syringe yet, do I?"

"You are correct. I have been informed that initial screening did not detect any relevant compounds. The samples are to be analyzed by more advanced and lengthy methods. The results will be available in due course."

"When?"

"A definite timescale cannot be set for the detailed procedure, but it will not be completed today."

At the terminus, Luke swept his identity card past the reader and gave the address of the Experimental Technology Institute where Libby Byrne's partner worked. As he got into a cab, he said to Malc, "Don't contact them to tell them I'm on my way. I want to surprise Royston Klein."

Chapter Twenty

The surprise paid off. When Luke arrived unannounced in Royston's workshop, the engineer froze for a moment. Taken aback, he tried to gather up and hide a sky-blue tracksuit from on top of a workbench. Realizing that he couldn't do it quickly enough, he gave up and pretended instead to move it casually as if it wasn't important.

Luke noticed his reaction but pretended that he didn't. "Sorry to burst in on you, but something's come up."

His eyes widened. "Is it Libby?"

"No, sorry. I want to ask you about shoes. Running shoes and ordinary ones."

Royston was still on edge, but he seemed to think that he'd avoided drawing Luke's attention to the tracksuit. "What do you mean?"

Luke glanced down at Royston's feet. "What size are yours?"

"Um . . . ten inches. Why?"

"Do you get athlete's foot?"

"In the past, yes."

"Recently?" said Luke.

Royston was clearly perplexed, but he wasn't panicking.

"No. Ages ago, I was plagued with it. It'd go away but kept coming back. Now I've got this stuff that I put between my toes, and it doesn't . . . What's this all about?"

"What stuff is that?"

Royston shrugged. "I don't know what's in it, but it works."

"I don't suppose you've got any with you."

"No," Royston answered. "I put it on every morning. At home."

"Including today?"

"Without fail."

"In that case, I'd like you to sit down and take your shoes and socks off. My mobile's going to scan your feet and socks for the powder."

Royston frowned. "I don't know what you're getting at, but it isn't a powder. It's a cream."

Luke still wanted to pursue the idea. "Even so . . ." Luke nodded toward Royston's shoes.

With a resigned sigh, Royston sat down and pulled off his shoes and black socks.

"Turn the socks inside out, please."

When Luke saw the material, he got a sinking feeling because he could not see any white flecks on the black wool. He asked Malc to scan Royston's socks and feet and then told Royston that he could put his shoes back on.

Luke looked around the workshop area, still ignoring the light-blue tracksuit. "Do you get involved with high-tech running shoes?" he asked.

Pulling the Velcro tab over the top of his right foot to fasten the shoe, Royston replied, "Personally, no. The institute does."

"I heard about this weird three-dimensional printing to make new shoes."

"That's right. We do it. It's very specialized at the moment, but one day all training shoes will be made like that. We call it laser sintering because that's what we do to build up an exact shape from specks of plastic."

"Do you supply athletes with these shoes?"

Royston stood up again. "I'm not sure. It's not my area. But it's a brand-new technology so they won't be in circulation much. Maybe a few prototype pairs are out there for testing. I think that we're concentrating on soccer cleats first."

Malc's neutral voice pronounced, "The subject's toes are smeared with chlorphenesin, but there is no zinc oxide dust."

"Thanks, Malc," Luke replied. It was the negative result that Luke was expecting. Trying not to break his concentration, he walked over to Royston's workbench. "You're into haptic clothing, aren't you?"

Royston began to look uneasy again. "You know that."

Luke picked up the sky-blue uniform and dangled it by the shoulders. It was heavier than he anticipated, probably because of the many sensors built into the material. "A bit small for you or me. Maybe it would fit—I don't know—a small girl. A gymnast, perhaps."

Royston lowered his eyes and said nothing.

"You told me that haptic clothing was all about monitoring health, but this shade of blue is Yvonne Chaplow's team color. So, I'm guessing that there's a sports application as well."

Still Royston stayed silent.

"I'm also guessing that it's not allowed. That's why you're anxious about the Games," Luke said. He could tell from Royston's expression that he'd hit the target. "You're helping athletes cheat. How does it work? How did a bit of cloth make Ford Drayton into a perfect runner? Come on. You might as well come clean now that I've gotten this far. I could get Malc to look through your computer records, and no doubt he'd find sports gear designed for members of Yvonne Chaplow's team."

"All right," Royston replied grudgingly. He shook his head, realizing that he was in a defenseless position. "It's true. Give athletes haptic clothing, and they've got all the feedback they need to fine-tune their performance."

"During a race or just in training?"

"It's up to them. A marathon runner wouldn't wear it for a race. It's hardly normal gear for distance, is it? But a gymnast or rower wouldn't stand out."

"What exactly does it do?"

"It's a great training tool. When the athlete has it on,

the tactile signals go into a computer for analysis. A coach can prompt whoever's wearing it to use specific muscles more, change a rhythm, or whatever. But there's a better way. I've put vibrating pads in them for automatic feedback. If the computer senses poor body movement or posture, it shakes the pad against the under-performing part, alerting the athlete right away. That way, they make a correction before bad habits set in."

"It's like having a trainer on your shoulder, telling you what to do all the time."

Royston nodded. "Yes. But much more efficient and precise." Trying to justify what he was doing, he added, "You're wrong about one thing. It hasn't been declared legal or illegal yet."

"So, right now, it's wrong. And it'll always be banned from tournaments because coaching isn't allowed once an event has started." Luke gazed into Royston's face and said, "No wonder you're jumpy about the Games. It might be Libby that you're worried sick about, but it's getting caught over this stuff that's really on your mind." Luke also understood why Saskia Frame had blushed when Yvonne claimed that her big secret was merely better-designed shoes.

"What are you going to do?"

Thinking, Luke drew in a deep breath. "You know, sports have to be fair. Otherwise it's more a test of technology than a competition between people. Either

nobody has an advantage like this or everybody does. I don't mind which, as long as it's a level playing field."

Royston repeated his question. "So what are you going to do?"

Luke turned to his mobile. "Malc?"

"Clarify your inquiry."

"What have you done with this information?"

"I have sent it to The Sporting Authorities, as required by my programming."

Facing Royston again, Luke shrugged. "It's out of my hands. But, if I were you, I'd stop cooperating with Yvonne Chaplow right away. Until the regulations catch up with the technology, my guess is that her team will be penalized, maybe even disqualified. That's tough on them—sad, really—but you have to think of all the other competitors, don't you?" He paused before adding, "I think that you agree with me. Otherwise, you wouldn't be jittery and your heart rate wouldn't have gone up last week when I mentioned the Games."

Royston Klein didn't reply, but he bowed his head.

Leaving the Experimental Technology Institute, Luke said to his mobile, "Actually, I don't want The Sporting Authorities to do anything about Yvonne Chaplow yet."

"Explain your reasoning."

"Simple. I'm not convinced that it's a good idea to upset her. If she's Spoilsport, she'd step up her campaign, and no one wants that. It'd be best to leave it until I have Spoilsport."

"Transmitting that advice to The Sporting Authorities."

"Just because her uniform socks are white, it doesn't mean that her people don't have other colors. Saskia's got a sky-blue scarf, so why not sky-blue socks?"

"Your reasoning is valid."

"It'd take me forever to get fibers from every suspect's socks. There's Saskia Frame, Yvonne Chaplow, Royston Klein and Libby Byrne, Frank Russell, Holly Queenan, Brooke Adams, and Venetia Murray. That's a lot of socks. So I want agents to do it—like you arranged for Trevor Twigg. They need to look for evidence of that antifungal powder as well."

"It may not be necessary to sample Venetia Murray's socks," Malc replied.

"Oh?"

"When I searched this subject's medical notes for athlete's foot, I discovered that she suffers from vertigo."

Luke hesitated and then smiled. "I see what you're getting at. She's not going to go up on scaffolding to undo bolts."

"Confirmed."

"Okay. Take her off the list."

"Transmitting request for remaining suspects."

Malc primed his laser and insisted on entering the Hounslow Residential apartment first, but there was no sign of another threat to Luke's life. Luke stripped off his

coat and then went to the mirror. His various bruises had lightened to a yellow-green color, hardly visible on his brown skin. The decomposition of hemoglobin had progressed to the stage of bile pigments, and soon his blood would carry them away. He smiled. It was impossible to set a timescale for the fading of bruises. They disappeared much quicker on young people and healthy adults than they did on the elderly. Sometimes, the color of old people's bruises lingered for months. That was one reason why, as an FI, Luke could never use the color of bruises to figure out when a victim had been beaten.

The gashes in his cheek and neck did not look as inflamed and swollen now. Both seemed to have been sewn nicely, like a professional repair of a torn pocket. The small scabs on the rest of his face, hands, and arms were beginning to peel away. He still looked a little like a pincushion, but he was no longer racked with aches and pains. He was simply more drained than normal.

"Connection to Jade," he said to Malc as he slumped into a chair across from the telescreen. He hoped that Jade would chase away his tiredness.

It was clear that returning to the North suited her. She looked bubbly, and she'd had her hair dyed the patchy color of rust. She looked so different that, if Luke hadn't known better, he could have imagined that she was the sister of the girl who'd said good-bye to him last night.

Beaming out from the telescreen, she said, "Hi. Listen

to this. It's just the opening bars of the anthem." Her hand stroked the strings of the electric guitar in her lap, and a loud, solitary refrain rocked Luke. Somehow, it was towering and plaintive at the same time. "That's all I've got so far. Solo guitar with a touch of feedback to add guts. I'll mix in other instruments once that has everyone's attention. It'll build slowly over a few minutes. From a solitary cry to complete clamor. That's what I'm aiming for. It's supposed to suggest one athlete joining other competitors, or athletes coming together into a national team, or even the stadium filling. Not very subtle, but it'll be startling."

"Breathtaking," Luke said.

She continued to nurse the guitar but peered at Luke. "How's things? Are you okay?"

"Fine. No one else has tried to flatten me. Or Malc."

"Yeah, well. Make sure that they don't get another chance."

"I just wanted to see that you got back okay . . ."

"Out of Spoilsport's reach, eh?"

Luke nodded. "Yeah."

"I've got a gig tonight. In a Barnsley nightclub."

"Enjoy it."

Jade smiled at him. It was a wistful wish-you-were-here smile. "You take care."

The screen faded to gray, and Luke closed his eyes. At least he didn't have to worry about Jade's safety anymore.

Chapter Twenty-One

It was late on Tuesday evening when Malc received the first results from The Authorities' agents and the forensic laboratory. "Trevor Twigg has one pair of sky-blue woolen socks that match the fibers found in the site manager's work shoes," he told Luke. "However, the material is common, so the match may be coincidental. There were no traces of zinc oxide and chlorphenesin adhering to any of this suspect's socks."

Fully dressed, Luke was resting on the bed with his fingers interlocked behind his head. "Pity."

"The findings do not prove his innocence or his guilt."

"True. Do you have any other feedback yet?"

"Yes. Neither Frank Russell nor Holly Queenan has socks that match the found fibers, and none had residues of the antifungal powder. A podiatrist has examined Brooke Adams. Blistering and irritation are common to athlete's foot and chemical poisoning, making diagnosis unsound."

Fighting against the weight of his eyelids, Luke replied, "Don't you have anything positive to tell me?" Not even the conversation with Jade had managed to revive him. He fell into a deep sleep before he absorbed Malc's negative answer.

* * *

There was little warmth in the sunlight that shone over the Aquatic Center and into the middle of Hounslow on Wednesday. But it was very bright. Luke screwed up his eyes as he walked toward the clinic where Brooke Adams was still a patient. At first, he didn't see the figure standing by a great big hole in the ground because the man's motionless frame was lost in the glare.

Malc began to alert Luke to his presence at the same moment that the man turned to scurry away. The movement caught Luke's attention. "Stop!" Luke yelled, shading his eyes with a hand on his brow. "Forensic investigator!"

There was no need. In an attempt to get away from Luke, the intruder ran straight into the arms of two burly builders. He muttered an apology and then turned to face Luke.

"You're a long way from home," Luke said to Trevor Twigg. "What brings you here at this time of the morning?"

"I came to see the latest mess-up." Trevor pointed along the trench that had been dug yesterday from the airstrip to the heart of the development. "It's a scar. And this . . ." He ran out of words when he pointed to the hollow that had been gouged for the foundations of the autocarrier station.

"What's wrong?" Luke asked.

"Don't you see?" he snapped. "This is pure vandalism of the past. There was a lot of archeological evidence here."

"Now that they've dug it out, can't you study what you want?"

171

The cavern was crisscrossed with steel rods that would strengthen the concrete when it was poured in.

Trevor was so angry that he was almost shouting. "What? You investigators drop history much too early in school. This is an excavation in the same way that a bomb's a way of stripping wallpaper from a house. It destroys more than it reveals. Proper digs are slow and painstaking."

Luke glanced down at Trevor's shoes. They were lighter than the reinforced footwear of a construction worker. "You were going to run away from me. Why?"

"No reason. I just didn't think that I'd be welcome."

"I have physical evidence linking you to a violent protest."

"I doubt that."

"I'm not going to arrest you," Luke said. "Not yet."

Trevor's laugh was malicious. "I thought that you'd have trouble landing that skate. Sounds like you're getting desperate."

The roof and guttering of Hounslow Medical Center were nearing completion, but the final touches seemed to generate more noise than ever. Brooke Adams was sitting in a chair next to her bed and watching the screen of a computer terminal that had been wheeled into the gangway. The color and texture of her face must have improved, because the normal skin around each eye did not stand out so much. Yet she still appeared rough and wrinkled, red and blue. Her tongue was clearly sore, but it was much less bloated. Her speech was unmistakably clearer.

"You look a lot better," said Luke.

She nodded and smiled. "I feel it." She hesitated before adding, "But you look like you've been through a hard time as well."

Luke shook his head. "It's nothing."

Brooke took a last glance at the sport on the monitor—some swimmers on their final length—and then turned it off with a sigh. "I'm not sure that I'll be back in a pool any time soon. Even if I could . . ."

"What?" Luke asked.

"It's all in the mind," Brooke said. "I'm not sure that I'd have the confidence . . . you know. I'd be worrying about the water more than swimming. A psychiatrist is trying to straighten me out, but . . ."

"At least you want to get back into it. Good for you."

"If I do, it'll be too late."

"Too late for what?"

Brooke answered, "The Youth Games, of course."

"What event would you have done?"

"One hundred and two hundred meters breaststroke."

Luke nodded sympathetically. "What were your chances? There aren't many surprises in swimming. It normally works out according to personal bests, doesn't it?"

"I'd be up for a medal in the one hundred meters. Maybe just miss out in the two."

Somewhere outside, there was a bout of hammering.

"Is Yvonne Chaplow your coach, by any chance?"

"I know that she's trying to recruit some swimmers—promising to improve their PBs—but, no, she's not mine."

"What type of swimmer are you? Do you look forward to races for the opportunity to win, or do you dread them in case you let yourself down? Is it the joy of winning or the dread of losing that fires you up?"

Brooke stared at him for a moment. "You're into sports, aren't you? You know how awful it feels to lose."

"Yes. I'd do anything to avoid losing," he lied. "What about you?"

"I know what you mean. But don't get me wrong. I love competing. It's just that . . . it's tough if your form's off or you know that you're not going to win."

Luke had learned what he'd come to find out. If Brooke believed that she was not going to do well in the Games, she might prefer the swimming to be canceled rather than put on a bad performance. She might welcome the excuse of an injury. "Hey," he said, looking at his watch, "I'd better leave you in peace or your doctor will tell me off. Look after yourself."

"Have you caught him yet?"

"The one who poisoned the water? No. But I'm closing in on him—or her."

In the pit that would soon become the foundation of the autocarrier station, the interlocking metal rods looked like a bizarre jungle gym. Instead of assembling the playground apparatus from the ground upward, the builders had sunk it down into the ground. The oblique sunlight could not penetrate every corner of the deep hole. Luke thought that he heard a whimper from the gloom. If there was something small but alive down there, he hoped that it could get out before the cavity was filled with wet concrete. Otherwise, it would suffer a horrible death.

"What's down there, Malc?" he asked.

Malc did not need floodlighting to probe the cavity. "It is a network of steel . . ."

"I mean, is there anything alive?"

Malc hesitated while he completed his scan. "A fox and a Nile monitor lizard. The fox has injuries consistent with falling through the steelwork, and the lizard appears to be unwell."

"Call in the vet," Luke said. "Maybe he can do something. I'd hate to think about them getting covered in concrete."

"The lizard would not suffer in the way that a human would . . ."

"Just send a message to Ian Pritchard. There's an old man who'd be delighted to see a Nile monitor

175

lizard if it can be saved."

"Transmitting. I have also received several significant reports on the suspects."

Luke turned away from the pit and stood to one side while a construction vehicle drove past. "Let's hear them. And I hope that there's something positive this time."

Malc replied, "It is all negative. No matching fibers or antifungal treatments have been discovered on the socks of Yvonne Chaplow, Saskia Frame, Royston Klein, Libby Byrne, or Brooke Adams. Podiatrists failed to diagnose athlete's foot on Yvonne Chaplow, Saskia Frame, Royston Klein, Trevor Twigg, Frank Russell, and Holly Queenan."

For a moment, Luke was stunned. "What you're saying is that I've just lost all of my major suspects."

"Incorrect. They remain suspects, but you have failed to find evidence against them at this point." Unlike Luke, Malc was not agitated by the setback. "I have been sent another result, but it is not valid for case notes because it cannot be linked to a suspect or a victim."

"What is it?"

"An extensive analysis of the soil samples taken from the cab terminus has been completed. No drugs were detected in the soil under the syringe barrel or in the water used to clean it. However, there were small clumps of clay inside of the barrel. Clay has the property of binding with many organic compounds. When these substances were freed from the clay, mass spectrometry revealed two drugs: tiletamine and zolazepam."

Feeling upbeat again, Luke said, "I've never heard of them. What are they?"

"Tiletamine is an anesthetic, and zolazepam is a tranquilizer. Together they are called Telazol, which is used to immobilize large animals. At its usual concentration, ten milliliters of Telazol is enough to tranquilize a polar bear."

Luke frowned for a moment and then grinned. "It's cold but not *that* cold. I haven't seen any polar bears."

"I refer to polar bears as an example of large animals," Malc replied without a hint of impatience. "Telazol has also been used to immobilize seals, rhinoceroses, horses, and hippopotamuses while veterinary operations are performed or tagging devices are attached."

Luke thought about it for a few seconds. "Would *people* use this drug?"

"No. It is not licensed for use on humans. It is considered to be too powerful. It is restricted to veterinary applications."

"All right. I need to see my darts-playing friend. Has Ian Pritchard received that request to come here?"

"His computer has registered the call out, but the veterinary surgeon is currently carrying out an operation at his clinic."

Luke fingered the lumpy scar on his cheek. "Take me there."

Chapter Twenty-Two

The animal clinic was housed in a small property, but at least it was in reasonable condition. Behind it, there was flat, open countryside. Nothing like the spectacular scenery of the North. Some trees formed a screen for a small crematorium, and the garden was a fitting and peaceful destination for the ashes of pets that had come to the end of their lives. By the time Luke entered the office, Ian had finished treating one of his patients and was seated at his computer terminal. When Luke opened the door, Ian closed the program and turned toward his visitor. "Ah. I was just reading your message," he said. "A wounded fox and an uncared-for lizard, is it?"

Luke nodded. "Do you know where the moving walkway's going to end?"

"Yes."

"You'll have to climb down to them, I guess."

Ian smiled. "It won't be the first time I've had to clamber around. Up trees, down holes, under cabs, in sewers. And you've seen me with an arm under floorboards." He shrugged. "I've done it all."

"Do you use Telazol?"

"Not on a fox, no."

"I mean, generally."

"Of course. It's my standard for immobilizing hefty

animals if I have to. Why?"

"I found some. By Hounslow cab terminus. It must be yours."

Ian hesitated for a moment and then nodded knowingly. "I wondered where it'd gone. I was on my way to Battersea Green Animal Sanctuary. They had a sick hippo. I lost a vial of Telazol en route."

"So you couldn't do the operation."

Ian shook his head. "I've learned from long experience to carry a spare of everything in case of hiccups."

Luke glanced at Malc, expecting him to object that a case of hiccups—even in a hippopotamus—would not require a surgical procedure, but he said nothing. Luke had forgotten that he'd added a new definition of "hiccup" to Malc's dictionary. His mobile now accepted that it could mean a mishap.

"It's not just me losing things," Ian continued. "Sometimes an animal doesn't react according to the instruction manual. I might've needed two tranquilizer darts to bring her down. Then again, I could've missed with one dart. As it happened, everything was okay with the one dose I had left. Hippo back in business. Thick-skinned but lovely creatures."

For a moment, Luke felt glum again. Another clue that he thought was significant seemed to have a perfectly innocent explanation. But he hadn't run out of ideas yet.

"Well," Ian said, getting up, "I'd better go and rescue your fox and Nile monitor lizard. Or put them down if

they're too far gone. I hope not."

"I don't suppose you get asked to take care of lizards much."

"Plenty of people keep snakes, but fewer people keep lizards. But I'm something of a specialist in reptiles and amphibians. If there's a sick one, I'm normally the vet they ask to kiss it better."

Luke grimaced. "If this one's okay, you'd make William Underwood a happy man. He might even know its name. He lives in Ealing now, but his nurse—Venetia Murray—would come and collect it from you. If it's his."

"I'll see what I can do." Ian grabbed his coat. "I'd better tell the site manager what I'm up to. I don't want to be down there when they start to lay the foundations, do I? That wouldn't be much fun."

In need of new leads, Luke sat in front of the computer terminal in his own room. "I haven't really looked into rival companies that missed out on the building work, Malc. Log on and do a search for all of the companies that put in a bid but got rejected. There's a possible motive there." He sighed. "And check Neil Gladwin's files. Is there a rogue builder with a grievance? Has he or Libby refused a promotion or fired someone? Something like that could turn a worker into Spoilsport."

"Searching."

"Give me a list on screen when you've got it." He took a

deep breath, trying to come up with more ideas. "I suppose someone in sports might want to ruin the Games for another team. Maybe the plan's to destroy Ford Drayton's chances— and all Yvonne Chaplow's athletes—if Spoilsport knows that she's trying to cheat with haptic uniforms."

"It is more likely that Spoilsport would inform The Sporting Authorities."

Luke nodded. "Good point. I'm not exactly buzzing. That noise you can hear is me scraping the bottom of the barrel."

"I have not detected such a sound. Additionally, you do not have access to a barrel in here."

One by one, names of building businesses and architectural firms had begun to appear on Luke's screen. Each company was listed with its address and the name of the individual who had made the unsuccessful bid to regenerate Hounslow.

It was the name of the fourth entry that caught Luke's eye. The manager of one architectural firm was named Hugo Twigg.

"Hold on!" Luke almost shouted. "Hugo Twigg. Is that coincidence, or is he related to Trevor Twigg?"

"Searching."

Luke's heart raced while he waited for his mobile to check through The Authorities' birth register.

"Hugo Twigg is Trevor Twigg's twin brother."

"Interesting. I would've thought that they'd both become historians."

"In a way, that is correct. Hugo Twigg submitted a plan based on the history of the region. It included time for an

archeological study of the area. He proposed that the new buildings should regenerate the styles of bygone years. The scheme was turned down for a number of reasons. Given the starting date of the International Youth Games, the schedule was considered unworkable. Also, The Authorities want the venue to be state-of-the-art and not reflect old-fashioned ideals."

"That's it, then!" Luke cried. "No wonder Trevor hasn't said anything about his brother. I want to see both of them right away. Try and find out where they are."

Malc failed to confirm the task.

Surprised, Luke was about to turn to his mobile when the computer screen went blank. A second later, it started flashing two words in large, red letters. GAMES OVER.

Luke swiped his identity card through the reader and hit the ENTER key again and again. Nothing happened. Mystified and muttering to himself, he said, "You know what this is, don't you? Spoilsport knows that I'm on to him. It's a virus attack."

Unusually, Malc did not voice his own conclusion.

Finally, Luke looked over his shoulder. To his amazement, his mobile was lying on the floor like a dead animal. The small red light that always flashed in Malc's metal casing had gone out. Mouth open, Luke asked, "What's going on?"

Malc did not reply.

Chapter Twenty-Three

The virus had sabotaged every computer in the area. The sports stadium control and timing system, LAPPED equipment, Hounslow Residential's workstation, the entire building site's network. And Malc. To Luke, his computerized mobile was by far the most important victim of the virus.

Aghast, Luke mumbled, "Now what do I do?" Without Malc, he was barely an FI at all. Without Malc to record and observe and analyze, there could be no case, no investigation. Without Malc, Luke couldn't even communicate with The Authorities and alert them to his situation.

He presumed that, somewhere in an office at the Houses of The Authorities, an alarm was ringing. He *hoped* an alarm was ringing. He knew that The Authorities kept track of all Mobile Aids to Law and Crime. They recognized when a fault developed. Luke had to trust that Malc had reported the virus attack in the instant before his programs failed. If he hadn't been able to send out a distress signal, Luke had to hope that a siren would sound within The Authorities' headquarters whenever a mobile went off air.

Without a computer that would respond to him, Luke was also helpless to counteract the virus. He relied on The Authorities to know what was happening and to send a technician to debug the whole system.

For now, Luke was alone, unprotected, and unable to carry out his job. He couldn't follow up his most promising lead. He had no way of finding out if the Twigg brothers were behind the sudden attack.

Having lost his link to the rest of the world, Luke felt trapped in his room. But going outside would be dangerous without the security that Malc provided. Also, it would be dark soon, and his mobile would not be there to light his way. Luke glanced again at Malc, but he was still powerless, just a lump of metal sprawled uselessly on the floor. Clearly, the virus had mangled his operating system.

It was no good. Luke could not simply sit and wait like a prisoner in a holding cell. Maybe The Authorities would expect him to lie low until agents could reach him, but Luke thought that he was vulnerable if he stayed where he was. Spoilsport had already attacked him in his own room. Anyway, Luke had no guarantee that agents were on their way. He had no guarantee that cabs were working in the Hounslow area. The computer virus might have wiped out their automatic-pilot programming. If cabs *were* still running, Spoilsport was just as likely to arrive as The Authorities' agents. Leaving Malc, Luke opened the door, peered down the empty passageway, and slipped out.

A mobile crane was lifting sawed-off chunks of the conifer away from the accommodation block and stacking them safely to one side. It was an easy job that didn't need a working computer.

As Luke made his way past the indoor arena, a builder shouted gruffly at him, "Who are you?"

Luke realized that without his constant companion, he was no longer instantly recognizable as an FI. He held out his identity card. "Luke Harding."

Clearly harassed, the construction worker peered at the card. "Forensic investigator? Are you sure? You don't look old enough."

"I'm on my way to see Neil Gladwin."

Still suspicious, the man in the hard hat said, "Without a Mobile Aid to Law and Crime?"

Luke nodded. "Computer glitch."

"Ah. That's why it's not a good idea to speak to Neil. Computers!"

Before Luke continued toward the manager's trailer, he noticed Saskia Frame emerging from the arena. She was blowing her nose into a blue handkerchief. The gymnast spotted him, came to a halt, and leaned against one of the huge pillars with a frown on her face.

There was a sharp crack to Luke's left, and out of habit he asked, "What was that?" He looked over his shoulder, but this time there was no one there to answer. He cursed the edginess that was threatening to grip him. No doubt, noises like that were perfectly normal on a construction site.

A small flock of pigeons took off from the roof of the indoor arena and headed into the darkening sky as if they were abandoning a scary setting. Ahead, the giant arms of the wind turbines rotated evenly, unconcerned with computer viruses and saboteurs.

Luke looked again at the entrance to the arena, but the gymnast was gone. She was nowhere to be seen.

Luke was aware that Spoilsport's latest piece of mischief might simply be an attempt to cripple the regeneration scheme through its computer system. He was also aware that it could be much more sinister. Knocking out the network might be just the first step of a more serious strike. If Spoilsport thought that the investigation was getting too close, the real target would be Luke.

The door of the manager's office wasn't locked, so Luke went right in.

Neil Gladwin was mumbling to himself. He banged the central desk with his fist so violently that the keypad leaped off the surface.

"Well, you've answered one question," Luke said.

Neil barely looked up. "What's that?"

"Your system's down as well."

"Yes," he snapped. "Games over! Very funny. This wouldn't have happened if you'd arrested him."

Luke ignored the insult. "Are electric cabs still coming and going, do you know?"

"I sent someone to find out. Yes. They're about the only thing that works around here."

"Did you see Ian Pritchard today?" Luke asked.

"Who?"

"The vet."

"Ah. Yes. He said something about rescuing an animal from where the autocarrier station's going to be." He shook his head and sighed. "Rescuing! He should be spending his time exterminating."

"You haven't laid the foundations yet, then?"

"Not with a vet down there," Neil replied impatiently. "He said that he'd be out of my way by the end of the day, so I logged the job for first thing tomorrow morning. Not that I can get into the log now," he grumbled. "What a disaster!"

"I'll leave you to it," said Luke.

"Get whoever's making my life a misery," Neil called after Luke, "before I murder him myself."

Nightfall sucked the remaining warmth out of the air. In the cold, clear sky, the full moon glowed brighter and brighter. The number of glittering stars multiplied while the workforce streamed away from the development. Many of the builders headed for Hounslow Residential. The rest went to the terminus for cabs.

Luke did not linger for long at the Aquatic Center or the clinic, but once again he paused by the deep hollow when he reached the end of the channel that had been cut for the autocarrier. For some reason, he felt uneasy about it. Perhaps he was concerned because he'd sent the vet down there. Luke didn't have a hope of seeing anything at the bottom of the hole. It was pitch-black down there. Leaning over it, he could barely make out the steel cage. "Hello?" he called into the emptiness.

Of course, there was no response. Ian Pritchard must have left long ago.

Something fluttered over Luke's head and made him jump. It took him a few seconds to figure out what Malc would have recognized immediately. Some bats were flying around and around in a circle, probably catching airborne insects that had been lured by the moonlight.

Looking around, Luke realized that he was now alone. The builders had all gone, but a few lamps were still on around the site. Above him were the comforting stars, the moon, and the ominous circling of bats. He shivered. At least there was still enough light to guide him back to the residential block. If he delayed any longer, though, it would be treacherously dark.

There was a quiet rustling near the ground a few feet away. It could have been a snake or a squirrel or some other creature with better night vision than his own.

Telling himself not to be silly, he set off again.

Almost immediately, he felt a sharp prick in the calf of his right leg. For an instant, he imagined that a snake had struck right through his pants. But, before his heavy eyes shut and he crumpled helplessly, he caught sight of something on the ground that told him exactly who Spoilsport was. In the moment before he lost consciousness, he knew with certainty and dread what had happened to Libby Byrne—and what was going to happen to him.

Chapter Twenty-Four

A trainee member of staff put her head around the door of the site manager's office in Hounslow Residential. "We've gone from room to room. Everyone's okay. But we found a Mobile Aid to Law and Crime in one apartment. It's had it."

The manager shrugged. "That'll be Luke Harding's. Any sign of him?"

"No."

"Just leave it, then. I've got my own chaos to sort out."

The trainee hesitated. "Shouldn't we tell The Authorities?"

The manager waved a despairing hand toward his computer. "And how am I going to do that?"

Behind the worried member of staff, a small, young woman coughed loudly and then briefly flashed her identity card. "No need to contact The Authorities. I'm a computer technician," she announced.

The manager didn't bother to look at the identity card. He simply leaped at the opportunity. "Come in!" he cried. "You can have a look at . . ."

The newcomer shook her head. "I heard you talking about Luke Harding's mobile. Take me to it, please. That's my priority." She let out a ferocious sneeze and cursed the cold weather.

It was almost midnight before Jade's computer in Sheffield managed to make a connection to Luke's mobile. But when an image appeared on her telescreen, it wasn't Luke. It was merely a mobile. Frowning, Jade asked, "Is that you, Malc?"

"I am Luke Harding's Mobile Aid to Law and Crime," he answered.

Taken aback, Jade said, "Where's Luke? What's happened?"

"Luke Harding has vanished."

Jade gasped. "What?"

"Luke Harding has vanished."

"But . . . what are you doing about it?"

"I am waiting for The Authorities to supply an FI to investigate the disappearance," Malc replied with maddening calm.

"No! You'll get out there and look for him, Malc. He's your friend."

"I am a machine. I do not have friends, and I am not programmed to operate on my own. I must have direction from a forensic investigator or from The Authorities."

"What's your top priority, Malc?"

"Upholding the law."

"All right," Jade said. "What's your second?"

"Protecting Luke Harding."

"Exactly. He might be hurt, Malc. You have to go and find him. It might be too late by the time you get reinforcements."

"That is valid reasoning."

"Luke's always working on a lead. His latest one would be a good place to start."

"Before a computer virus stopped my systems, he identified a new and strong suspect."

"Get on with it, then," Jade urged him.

"Not all of my resources are operational following physical damage and electronic assault. In particular, my range of scans is limited to standard infrared, visible, and low-power ultraviolet radiation."

"Look. When Luke got injured, did he stop working until he was fully recovered?"

"No."

"So you owe it to him to do the same."

"Processing."

"Good." Jade jumped up. "With a bit of luck, I'll meet you in Hounslow in a couple of hours or so."

"I am not programmed . . ."

"Shut up, Malc. Luke calls me his assistant forensic investigator, doesn't he? The best way to find missing people is to team up with someone who cares about them. I'm on my way."

Malc understood the principle of friendship. It was a state of mutual kindness between human beings, independent of family or romantic love. It offered pleasurable companionship and shared esteem. A form of friendship

191

could also occur between a person and a pet. Malc could not participate in such a relationship, but he recognized the need in law to discover and defend Luke Harding.

He did not understand the bond between Luke Harding and Jade Vernon, but it was evidently strong. If Luke Harding died, Jade Vernon would be disappointed even though very many other potential friends were available to her. Despite this, she acted as if Luke Harding was special and irreplaceable. As a result, Malc agreed that she was well motivated to find him. He told himself to welcome her assistance when she arrived in Hounslow.

With the virus banished from most computers and power restored, Malc logged on to the network and conducted a search. He needed to establish the location of each of the suspects.

Brooke Adams; swimmer; confirmed in Hounslow Medical Center.

Libby Byrne; first site manager; victim or suspect; whereabouts unknown.

Yvonne Chaplow; athletics coach; whereabouts unknown.

Saskia Frame; gymnast; whereabouts unknown.

Neil Gladwin; second site manager; confirmed at work on computer in manager's headquarters.

Royston Klein; Libby Byrne's partner; engineer; confirmed at home.

Venetia Murray; nurse; thought to be at home.

Holly Queenan; bandit, protester, and suspect; whereabouts unknown, likely to be in Hounslow.

Frank Russell; protester and suspect; whereabouts unknown, likely to be in Hounslow.

Hugo Twigg; historical architect; thought to be in Birmingham.

Trevor Twigg; historian; thought to be in Brighton.

William Underwood; retired biologist; confirmed at home.

Unable to come to an unambiguous conclusion, Malc examined an aerial map for the Hounslow development. He calculated that a wide infrared scan of the entire area, looking for the characteristic warmth of a human being, would take two hours and seven minutes.

Malc compared the merit of scanning for two hours and seven minutes with the option of stalling until an alternative forensic investigator arrived. The search might achieve the desired outcome of finding Luke Harding, while waiting would waste time. On that basis, he made his decision.

When Malc slid the door open via its electronic control and made his way out of the building, it was the first time that he had acted under his own initiative.

He started the scan at the cab terminus on the eastern side. Rising to a height of ten feet above the tallest object below him, Malc turned on his wide infrared beam and slowly drifted toward the site manager's office on the

extreme west. He had to change his elevation when he came across the Aquatic Center, medical center, and indoor arena. Of course, he could only scrutinize the outside of the structures, but he had already checked that FI Harding's card had not been used to enter any of the buildings since the time of the virus attack. If Luke Harding was still on the site, it seemed likely that he would be outdoors.

At the end of an unsuccessful sweep, Malc moved slightly north and began a second run from west back to east. This time, he had to rise to the highest altitude and hover very slowly to survey the entire main stadium. His search gave a positive result. There was a human-shaped, red-yellow glow walking between the seats in the completed south stand. As Malc fixed on to the signal, he did not feel hopeful or excited, because he could not feel hope or excitement.

Avoiding the imposing arch, he swooped down for a closer scan that would define the shape more accurately. He also bathed the subject in visible light and compared the features with his database. The subject definitely matched Holly Queenan.

Because Malc did not have an investigator's direction, he did not consider stopping Holly Queenan and asking her some questions. He moved away and up, through a ring of bats using echolocation to pinpoint their prey, and continued his scan.

When he finished surveying the stadium, he dived down much closer to the ground. He drifted over the cavity where he had earlier detected a fox and a Nile monitor lizard at the request of his forensic investigator. This time, his scan did not reveal any living forms in the hole. He moved on toward the terminus again. As soon as he reached it, he turned and executed a third sweep.

After two hours and seven minutes, Malc was not cold, bored, or disheartened. Concluding the process at the cab terminus, he logged his failure to provide any valid data. He was about to run logic programs to decide if there was a rational next step when a lone cab pulled into the Hounslow loop.

Chapter Twenty-Five

In the early hours of Thursday morning, there was still no sign of Luke or a substitute investigator. Too fidgety to sit down or take off her coat, Jade stood in Luke's apartment. She felt more anxious than tired. She hadn't even managed to nap in the cab. Concern for Luke was keeping her awake and alert. "I know how his brain works," she said to Malc. "If he thought that someone was after him, he'd be pleased in a way. It'd mean that he was closing in on whoever did it. So, who was the last person he interviewed?"

"When considering specific details of a case, I respond only to Luke Harding," Malc replied.

Exasperated, Jade shook her head and looked around. "Where is he?"

"His current whereabouts are not known."

"Right. So, talk to his assistant instead."

"There is no such official position. The Authorities will not accept . . ."

"Think about it, Malc. Spoilsport released a computer virus—probably to knock you out—and then went for Luke. He'd only do that if he thought that Luke was a threat. If you want to get Luke back as much as I do, you don't have to tell The Authorities what you're up to. You just have to tell me who he spoke to last. Now would be a good time."

Malc hesitated for a split second before answering, "Ian Pritchard."

"Who's he?"

"A veterinary surgeon. He is not considered a suspect."

"What did Luke say to him?"

Malc did not explain their conversation. He simply played back his recording of it.

Jade listened carefully and then said, "If this man's not a suspect, why did Luke ask him if he used Telazol or whatever it was called? The tranquilizer."

"It is the role of a forensic investigator to direct interviews. I am not required to justify individual questions. However, Luke Harding appears to be establishing that the presence of Telazol and a syringe barrel at Hounslow cab terminus had an innocent explanation."

Jade shook her head. "Luke's never managed to hide anything from me. I can read his voice. When he said, 'So you couldn't do the operation,' he was suspicious. I can hear it, clear as can be. He was fishing for more information, wondering if this vet was telling the truth," she said. "What you've got to do now is check if there ever was a sick hippo at the animal sanctuary."

"It is highly unlikely that the keepers are available at this time."

"Malc! Set off their fire alarm. Get them up. I don't

care. Search their computer or whatever you do. Just get an answer. Has Pritchard done an operation on their hippo?"

Jade paced up and down impatiently for six-and-a-half minutes.

Then Malc announced, "I have confirmed that Battersea Green Animal Sanctuary has not requested any veterinary procedures on a hippopotamus for at least one year."

At once, Jade headed for the door. "Come on! We're going to this vet's place."

Dawn was still more than three hours away. Malc's metal coat was reflecting moonlight, and his small red light flashed faintly. The animal clinic was quiet and dark. Jade didn't have a clue what she was doing there, but she thought that the answer lay with the vet who had lied to Luke. She turned to Malc and whispered, "Let's try around the back."

Creeping quietly, she made her way around the house to the rear but came to a halt at the corner and sniffed the air. "What's that?" she asked, pointing to a small outbuilding with a screen of trees and smoke gently rising from its chimney.

"It is a pet crematorium."

At once, Jade froze. Her spine was tingling horribly, and the hairs on the back of her neck were standing up.

"FI Harding was aware of this facility. During a game

of darts, he asked the veterinary surgeon about disposal of animal remains."

Jade could barely speak. "I think I know why. It's a perfect cover for getting rid of . . ." She couldn't finish the sentence. She gulped and stared at the gray smoke drifting toward the black sky.

Insensitive to her distress, Malc said, "Cremation is a plausible way to remove almost all traces of a body."

"Does that mean . . . ? No! It can't be Luke!"

Malc closed in on the brick building, but the door was padlocked and there was no window. Instead, he glided across the garden.

"What are you doing?" Jade whispered urgently.

"I am scanning the ground for objects of significance."

"Why?"

"Because I am programmed to search out evidence of a crime."

Jade was horrified by Malc's cold-blooded response. "We're talking about Luke, not a crime!"

"My metal detector has located a buried watch, a pairing ring, and the hinges and metal clasps from a briefcase."

"So what?"

In his flat tone, Malc answered, "These concealed artifacts precisely match the items carried by Libby Byrne when she disappeared."

Jade opened her mouth to say something, but she found it hard to speak. She would never get used to Malc delivering an emotional punch with such composure. She took a deep breath and swallowed. "Is there anything belonging to Luke?"

"Nothing detected."

Jade looked around again and then crossed the lawn toward the back of the clinic where there was a door and a window. The grass deadened her footfalls, but the last two steps were on stones so she tiptoed. Cupping her hands around her eyes, she peered through the glass but could not distinguish anything inside.

The back door opened, making Jade jump. She cracked her head on the window and let out a pained "Ow!" Before she could recover from the shock, Ian Pritchard had grabbed her. His right arm pressed heavily and uncomfortably into her throat. In his left hand, he held some sort of metal instrument.

"You know what this is, don't you?" the vet said, waving the stubby rod that Jade had never seen before.

It was Malc who answered. "It is an electrical device used to stun animals before they are killed."

"Yes. So stay away or she gets it."

"I am not programmed to protect Jade Vernon."

For a moment, Pritchard was taken aback. "What? You're not an FI, then!"

Jade struggled to say, "No."

"Who are you?"

Jade knew better than to tell Spoilsport that she was

the Games' musician. He had a grudge against anyone connected with the sports project and, even now, Jade could hear the principal of the Sheffield Music Collective saying that she should think of herself as part of the Hounslow regeneration scheme. "I'm Luke's friend."

Ian looked back at the Mobile Aid to Law and Crime. "Aren't you programmed to protect an FI's friends?"

"Not without a specific instruction. In any event, my defensive systems have not resumed normal operations after the virus attack."

Jade could hardly believe it. Why was Malc such an honest simpleton? He'd left no scope for bluffing. Now Pritchard knew that Malc couldn't zap him with a laser or anything. Freed from danger, the vet could do anything to her. No wonder she could feel him chuckling silently to himself.

"What have you done to Luke?" she blurted out.

"He's a good darts player, isn't he? Pity."

"What have you done to him?"

Ian followed her gaze until he saw the chimney, and then he laughed aloud. "You think that's him, there. Reduced to a puff of smoke? Well, maybe you're right."

"No, you're just mocking me." Jade was confident because she listened to people's voices. She knew when they weren't telling the truth.

Pritchard tightened his arm around her neck. "You're right. He's an FI. That makes him special. He deserves a memorial."

"What do you mean?" Jade's indignant shout came out as a strangled croak.

Ignoring her, the vet stared at Luke's mobile. "If I know the rules, you can't do anything without an FI. Certainly not arrest anyone."

Uncharacteristically, Malc faltered before replying, "Correct."

"This is going to be easier than I thought . . ."

Playing for time, Jade said, "Tell me. Why are you doing all these things?"

For a few seconds, the vet was silent. Jade guessed that he was probably wondering if there was any harm in answering her question. "I heard what Harding's machine said. It has found Libby Byrne's stuff. That means it has evidence against me." He laughed quietly. "It won't matter when I destroy it and get rid of you. Anyway, I'll tell you because I'm proud of what I've done. Those idiot builders couldn't be bothered to wait for me to get to William Underwood's reptile house. They brought it down, crushing and killing the poor creatures." He paused, clearly still affected by the massacre of the old man's pets. "They did it to make an airport, so I brought one of their planes down to show them how it felt. That satisfied me for a while, but then the old anger came back. It nagged at me that I missed getting the woman who was responsible, so I brought down some of her buildings as well and got her at last. An animal tranquilizer when she turned up for work and cremation." He shook his head and snorted. "But that's not the end of it. The builders sprayed the place with toxic chemicals, even knowing that it deformed frogs, so I did the same in their swimming pool."

"What about Luke? What's he done? Nothing!"

"He was an FI. He was on their side."

Jade caught her breath when she heard the past tense. "*Was?*"

"He was on the verge of figuring it out. Very smart. I had to get rid of him."

"What have you done to him?"

Ian laughed again.

That was it. Jade wasn't prepared to take any more.

Chapter Twenty-Six

Without warning, Jade jabbed her elbow violently into the vet's stomach.

Momentarily winded, Ian stepped back.

That was a mistake, because it gave Jade the space that she needed. She took aim, swung her leg, and kicked him as hard as she could.

Ian gasped, groaned, and fell to the ground. He let go of the stun gun and curled up like a wounded animal.

Jade didn't know exactly what she was doing, but she headed for the back door. Perhaps Luke was hidden somewhere inside.

Malc followed her indoors and turned on the lamp.

At once, Jade was surrounded by cages and overwhelmed by the smell of animals. Some small cages contained wounded birds, gerbils, and hamsters. Bigger cages housed rabbits, an endangered cat, and a sick chimpanzee. The largest cage held an unwell panther. Then there were several sealed tanks teeming with reptiles and amphibians. Each enclosure had its own perfect atmosphere, with the humidity and temperature carefully controlled. So many snakes, lizards, frogs, and toads couldn't possibly all be sick, Jade thought. They were more likely to be Pritchard's pets than his patients.

Speaking over the whimpering and scratching sounds, Malc said, "I cannot encourage you to break the law, but a shotgun is propped behind the door. You may use it for self-defense, if required."

Jade got to it in time. She grabbed the rifle in both hands and readied it for firing just as the door opened and the vet staggered inside. Jade had used guns in sports at Birmingham School. But she still shook as she lifted the weapon and pointed it at Pritchard. She had never aimed one at a person before.

"Where is he?" she asked, her voice trembling.

Ian smiled. "I keep shotguns in case I have to put something down in a hurry to stop it from suffering. Is that how you think of me, eh? Do you want to put me out of my misery?"

"What have you done to Luke?" she snapped.

"I don't think you'll fire. You don't have what it takes to put anything down, do you?"

He was right, and he could probably see it in her eyes.

"Killing saps you," the vet said. "Believe me, I know. Rats, I don't mind, but anything else . . . Today, I had to kill a wounded fox by the stadium." He shook his head sadly. "Tragic. The builders' fault. It fell down their hole."

Jade wasn't sure what he was talking about, but she recognized someone who no longer cared what he did to other human beings. He'd given her an idea, though.

"You're right," she said. "I couldn't kill anyone, but . . ."

She swung the shotgun around and aimed it at the largest tank, a writing mass of snakes. "I'll tell you what I could do. I could blast your precious reptiles."

"No!" He stared first at Jade and then at the tank she was threatening to shatter.

"Where's Luke? That's what I want to know."

Ian did not reply.

She shuddered as she asked, "Have you cremated him?"

The vet shook his head.

"What, then?" Deliberately, she made sure that Pritchard could see her forefinger beginning to squeeze the trigger. Now there was nothing to be read in her eyes apart from determination.

"All right!" he snarled. "Don't hurt them. I'll tell you."

Not daring to relax, Jade said, "Go on, then."

"He's in the arena—where we played darts. I immobilized him with Telazol."

"What's that going to do to him?" Jade demanded to know.

Pritchard shrugged. He didn't care. "Byrne didn't come around. It's just as well, when you think about what happened after that."

Jade scowled at him. "You've got other plans for Luke. What?" She poked the rifle toward the reptile enclosure.

"He might not survive. If he does—if he wakes up— he's not going to last long. I doused the whole room with glycerol and nitric acid."

Keeping her eyes on the vet and the rifle trained on the reptile tank, she said, "Malc?"

"What is your inquiry?"

"What's he done to the room?"

"Mixing glycerol and nitric acid makes nitroglycerin. It is an unstable explosive that is sensitive to impact and friction."

"What are you saying?" she yelled. "If Luke steps on it, it'll go off?"

"Confirmed."

"A little chemistry comes in handy, doesn't it?" Ian said with a sneer.

Full of disgust for the vet, Jade snapped, "You're a monster." Then she took a deep breath. "Okay, Malc," she said. "We're going to rescue him. Somehow. But . . ." She nodded toward Pritchard. "What do we do with . . . ?"

Ian smiled. "It's a dilemma, isn't it? You want to go to your FI, and you want me locked up. But you can't have both, because it," he said, pointing at Malc, "can't do a thing without Harding. It can't even arrest me."

The mobile replied, "This house is surrounded by security guards."

"What?" Pritchard spluttered. "But . . ."

Surprising them both, a female voice emerged from Malc. "This Mobile Aid to Law and Crime has been streaming video to me—the Deputy Head of Criminology—ever since it discovered artifacts

belonging to the missing Libby Byrne. It has enabled me to take the place of a forensic investigator, and I am satisfied that there is sufficient evidence to charge Ian Pritchard with the murder of Libby Byrne, the mass murder of the passengers on Flight GGW17, and the malicious wounding of Brooke Adams. Further charges, relating to property damage, electromagnetic disruption, FI Luke Harding, and two deaths in Hounslow Stadium, are pending. I have authorized the arrest."

The door burst open, and before Jade could react, Ian Pritchard was surrounded. It all happened so quickly. The vet was bundled away, and a guard took the shotgun from her.

Jade was left with an empty feeling. There was a vacuum where Luke should have been.

In the cab, the same female voice said, "You have done well, Jade Vernon. The Authorities thank you. But it is now time for you to return to normal. A very experienced forensic investigator has been released from other duties. She is expected to arrive at eight-thirty to take over . . ."

"Eight-thirty!" Jade exploded. Outside, there wasn't even a hint of dawn yet. 8:30 A.M. seemed like a long away. "You heard what Pritchard said. Luke could wake up at any moment and . . ."

"I understand your concern, Ms. Vernon, but the task

ahead is very dangerous. It requires qualities and specialist skills that you don't have."

"But . . ."

"If the floor is coated with a substance that detonates on the impact of a shoe, how do you proceed?"

"I stay out and send Malc in."

"If FI Harding is immobilized, how do you wake him up?"

Still refusing to give in, Jade said, "He'll respond to my voice."

"And if he doesn't?" asked the detached voice of The Authorities.

Jade sighed. "I don't know."

"I have consulted a doctor. The effects of the tranquilizer on humans are not known, but it may be possible to reverse them by administering a drug called yohimbine. You are not qualified . . ."

Jade interrupted again. "Malc can do that if you give it to him."

The voice hesitated.

"And I have one quality that your FI doesn't have. The most important one."

"What's that?"

"I care about him," Jade said with sheer belief and grit.

After five seconds, the Deputy Head of Criminology replied, "All right. It is most irregular, but I will instruct this mobile to continue working with you."

"Thank you."

"Take care, Ms. Vernon. You're a musician. Remember that. Bear your limitations in mind. You must avoid all unnecessary risks. If you are in doubt at any time, you must consult with the mobile, who will be in contact with me."

"Okay."

"And, Jade?"

"Yes?"

"I wish you good luck."

Jade was flushed with her success in getting her own way, but once the effect wore off, she felt nervous and inadequate. She wasn't going to admit it, though. Not to The Authorities. Not even to an inanimate machine.

Chapter Twenty-Seven

Malc recharged his batteries as much as possible during the short journey. As soon as the electric cab came to a halt in Hounslow, he got out with Jade and led her through the deserted construction site. He stopped beside the four imposing pillars and the plinth without its statue. "This is the building," he told her. "I am instructed to confirm that you still wish to proceed."

"Just take me to the room," she said. She told herself that it didn't matter if Malc saw her quaking, but she did her best to hide it anyway.

There were no lights on in the eerily quiet building. It was Malc who lit the way. Only once did his beam pick out movement. A rat scurried along the passageway and then disappeared into a hole that would be an electrical socket once the interior had been completed.

Malc guided her past the gymnastics hall to a series of game rooms. The mobile halted outside of the second one. "This is the room in which Luke Harding and Ian Pritchard played darts."

Fearful of what she was about to find, Jade swallowed. Her heart seemed to be at the point of bursting. "Okay. Let's do it."

"There is no lock. You should push the door open

without going in. I will shine a light inside. Regardless of what you see," Malc said, "you must not enter the room. I am required to hinder your access."

"Deal," Jade replied.

When she reached out for the door, the sight of her own hand surprised her. It was quivering visibly in the light that was coming out of Malc. There was no hiding her fear now.

She pressed the button, and the door clicked open. She gave it a push, and it swung back easily, without a sound.

Malc went forward, blocking her way and flooding the room with light.

Behind him, Jade caught her breath. "What . . . ? Malc! What's going on?"

The game room was empty.

Malc did not seem perturbed. He said, "I am programmed to consider that suspects and culprits may not tell the truth. Ian Pritchard has deliberately given incorrect information."

"How can you just . . . ?" With her fists on her hips, she answered her own question. "Because you're a machine." She shook her head, annoyed but not beaten. "Now what?"

"A standard procedure for this situation does not exist."

On the steps outside, Jade watched the first rays of the sun and heard the first stirrings of the site. A few construction workers began to stroll past and greet each other with little enthusiasm for a new day. In her mind, she ran through every word of what Pritchard had said to her. She relied on her memory because she'd forgotten that she could ask Malc to play his recording. There was just one sentence that struck her as strange. "Pritchard said something about Luke deserving more than cremation. What was it?"

Within a few seconds, Malc retrieved the dialogue. "Referring to Luke Harding, the accused said, 'He's an FI. That makes him special. He deserves a memorial.'"

Jade frowned. "A memorial. Why did he say that?"

"Insufficient data."

"Do you have a dictionary, Malc?"

"Confirmed. I am equipped with . . ."

"Just give me all of the definitions of "memorial"."

Slowly, the rising sun illuminated Hounslow regeneration scheme. One building after another came into view. The long shadows all pointed west. Jade wished that they were giving her directions.

"Noun: something, chiefly in the form of a monument, sculpture, or other structure, that serves to preserve the memory of a person or event; a historical record; a memorandum or diplomatic communication; a statement of facts addressed to The Authorities. Adjective: of or involving memory . . ."

"All right," Jade said. To herself, she muttered, "A monument, sculpture, or other structure." She looked at the pillars and the plinth. "In other words, a memorial stone. That's it, Malc!" she cried.

"Explain."

"Is there anything that's about to be made out of concrete?"

"Yes. The foundations of the autocarrier station. A cavity has been prepared for filling."

"That's where he is. He's going to be buried under his own memorial stone!"

"Your speculation is incorrect. I have already scanned the cavity. There was no trace of a living, warm-blooded being."

"He's there! I know he is!" Jade insisted.

"There are no facts to validate that conclusion."

The first heavy motor chugged into life and revved up. The first of the day's jobs was beginning.

"Do you have a better idea?" Jade shouted at Malc.

"A logical deduction is not possible from the available information."

"It's my call, then. Come on!"

Following the shallow trench that would soon become a moving walkway, she ran toward the end of the line.

Chapter Twenty-Eight

To Luke, it felt more like a nightmare than like waking up. Briefly conscious, it took him a while to come to his senses. It was completely dark, and he thought that he saw stars. He must have been wrong, because he felt enclosed. There was weight on his body, all over, even on his face. He was cold and damp yet hot and sweating. Every single part of his body ached as if it had been pummeled relentlessly. He was incredibly weak. He wanted to groan, but his mouth would not move. He wanted to vomit but couldn't. The bile burned his throat and tongue like acid. He wanted to take big gulps of fresh air, but something stopped him from even doing that. He breathed through a partially blocked nose. He was unbelievably thirsty, but there was no water.

He wanted to brush the thing from his face, but he couldn't move his hands or feet. Instead, he strained his neck to lift his heavy head a few inches. Whatever the thing was, it wasn't solid. He wasn't trapped inside of a box. It was some sort of material that moved with him. He let his head fall again, and it came to rest on something soft. Not as soft as a pillow and not as hard as wood. But it was damp, so it wasn't a carpet. His head pounded. He was definitely dehydrated. Yet, under the weight of the material, he was sweating.

His brain cleared a little more, and he smelled animal. Horse maybe.

He tried again to move his hands and arms. He could flex his elbows and form fists with his fingers. No bones were broken. But when he tried to move his wrists, he realized that they were attached to something immovable. Narrow straps dug into his skin.

It was the same with his legs. He could rock his knees from side to side, but his ankles were attached to something. Under the blanket—yes, it was a bulky blanket his feet were clenched with cramps. He attempted to ease them by wiggling his toes.

He realized that he had his shoes on. And he was still wearing clothes.

He was outside. He didn't know exactly what told him. Maybe it was the air that he was sniffing. It was cold. And underneath his head, it was soil. But if he was outside, he would have been freezing. He wasn't. Sweat was soaking into his clothes.

It was a thermal blanket! It had to be. And it had been used to keep a sick animal warm, no doubt. That's why it smelled of horse.

A sick animal. A vet. Ian Pritchard.

He opened his eyes and turned his head painfully. In some sort of flashback—a trick of memory—he saw Ian's duffel bag, open, revealing a clear plastic bag and a dead rat. Then he felt that prick in his leg again.

Hippo tranquilizer. He couldn't recall the name of the drug. Not for human use. Too powerful. Too dangerous. That's why his body was calling for water—to flush out the remains of the tranquilizer. That's why he ached to be vomit—to get it out of his system. That's why, from head to toe, he was burning with pain.

His mouth was sealed with tape. He couldn't vomit. Couldn't cry out. Pritchard didn't want anyone to hear him. That meant that people might be nearby.

An idea formed in his mind, and for a moment, he panicked. Was he in Pritchard's pet crematorium? Luke was convinced that's how the vet had removed all traces of Libby Byrne. Excellent plan. How does a killer conceal the evidence of a dead body? He treats it like any other body and cremates it. Was that Luke's end as well? He shuddered at the thought that he might be conscious at the time.

No. He was wrong. He wasn't indoors. Not in a crematorium. No smell of burning or ashes.

He pulled on his arms and legs again, trying to free them, but there was no chance. He could feel what was happening now. There were plastic straps around his wrists and ankles. His skin was tight against cold metal. Metal rods.

In an instant of clarity, Luke knew everything. He remembered peering into the black pit. He'd called out because he was worried that the vet might be lying somewhere in the steel cage, a victim of Spoilsport.

That's when he'd felt the dart. Seen the duffel bag, the plastic bag, the dead rat. Luke was the victim. He was the one bound to the metal framework down in the hole.

He writhed around as much as he could, trying to rid himself of the blanket. He would have used his teeth—anything—to dislodge it if he could, but he couldn't. He knew why Pritchard had shrouded him with it. If Malc was repaired and scanned the site at night, he'd use infrared. Thermal imaging. Looking for body heat. Luke's signature warmth would be invisible under a thermal blanket. There would be no thermal image.

Luke floated in and out of awareness.

Was it morning? Was there light? It was so dingy in the pit that no one would notice a dark blanket covering a live human being. He would not be seen in daylight, either.

Luke froze. The foundations were going to be laid first thing in the morning! That's what the manager had said.

Luke was helpless and hidden. And tons of wet concrete were about to choke him. Crush him. Luke gulped back the foul and bitter taste in his sealed mouth. A little vomit dribbled out of his nose. Fighting the effects of the drug, he yanked on the plastic straps until they cut his skin, and the pain made him stop. He felt faint as the blood began to flow from his wrists and ankles.

He hated the thought of what was about to happen to him. Yet he himself had given Spoilsport—Ian Pritchard—the idea. The vet had watched him scanning the pillars of the indoor arena. Pritchard must have realized that Luke was looking for a body concealed in the concrete. In the vet's warped mind, there would be a perverse beauty in subjecting Luke to the fate that Luke himself had imagined.

Luke understood, but he could not react. And it was too late. He heard the engine approach. A cry formed in his stinging throat, but it died there because his lips were sealed together. The motor was dreadfully close, somewhere above him. It quieted down a little but did not stop. It was idling.

Voices. Human voices.

"Okay, let's get it done. Swing the chute over here. Aim at the middle," a bored voice said.

"Whoa! Not that far. Back a bit," an impatient voice responded.

"Right. She's in place. Let her go," an authoritative voice boomed out.

First it was a rattling noise, a grinding, thudding. The steel rods were vibrating against his limbs. Then there was a splashing noise. The awful sound in Luke's ears was concrete cascading into the pit.

Chapter Twenty-Nine

Jade was hurtling through the messy building site with Malc at her shoulder. When a group of construction workers appeared in front of her with huge drills and a trailer containing supports for the covered walkway, she waved her arms at them and shouted, "Out of the way!"

The team stopped and stared. They were too startled to move aside quickly.

"I'm a forensic investigator!" she roared.

That made them move. They pulled the trailer aside.

Malc attempted to correct her and state the law on the impersonation of an FI. "You must not . . ."

"Don't you start!" Jade cried, as she forced more effort from her legs and panted for air.

"The position of the autocarrier station is four hundred and twenty-six feet ahead."

It was like the final lap. Just a few seconds for a decent runner. But Jade was not an athlete.

She saw a huge rotating drum and a group of people in overalls and hard hats standing around a chute, looking into a hole in the ground.

Getting closer, she could see the gush of wet concrete. She gasped. At the top of her voice, she yelled, "Stop!"

"You do not have sufficient evidence to order a cessation . . ."

"Stop!" she repeated. "Forensic investigator!"

One of the builders looked up at her and, believing he'd been instructed to halt the operation by an FI, pulled a lever beside the chute. More of the gray slush slid down the metal channel and fell into the cavity, but the drum wound down to a standstill, and no more appeared at the top of the slipway.

Jade ignored the workers and came to a halt in a cloud of steamy breath at the edge of the pit. "Oh, no!"

A huge mound of watery sand, cement, and stones was standing in the middle of the pit. Easily enough to cover and suffocate anyone underneath.

Struggling for breath, she shrieked, "Malc!"

"The center of the cavity is already submerged," the mobile replied, telling her what was obvious. "I have scanned the edges and corners that are still exposed. I have detected . . ."

"What?" Jade snapped.

"A dead fox."

Jade stared at him. "A dead fox! Is that all?"

"Correct. There are items of garbage, cloths, and a section of tarpaulin, presumably blown into the hole by the wind . . ."

"Shush!" Jade muttered.

Leaning her head to one side, she strained to hear.

"What's that?" she said to herself.

"What are you referring to?"

"That noise."

"I have detected fourteen . . ."

Jade waved her arms at Malc and everyone else. "Shush!" she shouted. "I can't hear. Kill any noise. Stop that engine!"

With her hands on her hips, she waited for the sound to fade.

She was not going to get silence, not on a massive construction site that was still coming to life, but she had stunned everyone within earshot with the passion of her cry.

In the silence that followed, she listened intently.

And there it was.

Someone was emitting a strangled, out-of-tune hum.

It was muted and discordant, but it was the best sound that Jade had ever heard. It was recognizable as the opening bars of her sports anthem.

"It's him, Malc!"

"My voice recognition program has analyzed all current sound. Each human voice is unique, defined by muscles, vocal cavities, and the length, tension, and shape of the vocal cords . . ."

Jade paid no attention to him. She was prowling around the hole, peering into its depths. The weight of the fluid concrete was making the gray slush settle slowly. Soon, it would reach the edges and creep into all four corners, covering the entire bottom of the hole. Covering Luke.

Frantic, she cried, "Where is he, Malc? Where's the sound coming from?"

"The source of the hum is the northwest corner."

Jade looked up at him. "What?"

One of the builders interrupted. "It means that corner." He pointed.

"Right!" Jade knew what she had to do. Malc was too big to go through the network of steel rods, but she could use it like a ladder. She sat on the edge of the pit, grabbed the highest bar, and swung her legs down to make contact with one of the rungs.

Several of the construction workers shouted at the same time. "You can't do that! It's too dangerous."

She ignored them.

One man appeared above her as she began the descent. He put his arm out toward her and said, "Take my hand. Come on. I'll pull you up, or it'll be the last thing you do. Hurry! It's not stable."

He was right. The concrete was spreading like lava enveloping the side of a volcano.

"If you want to help," Jade said, "get me a crane or a winch or something." She flashed him a look of utter determination.

Malc said, "You must take wire cutters."

Jade paused. "Why?"

"Luke Harding is clearly conscious. If he was free to move, he would have climbed out himself. I deduce that he is secured in some manner."

A builder knelt at the edge of the foundations and held out some sturdy cutters. "Here. Take these."

Jade clutched them in her fist and continued to climb down. Malc hovered above and lit her way as the unstoppable sludge crept closer, little by little filling the cage.

Jade looked down. Only a few feet to go. Malc's illumination created a sinister pattern of light and shadow in the pit, but Jade could make out some sort of covering. That had to be it. As quickly as she could, she hurried toward it. The cumbersome wire cutters in her hand clunked on the steel poles each time she went down one step. Under her weight, some of the bars bent and the whole contraption creaked. It was designed to strengthen foundations. It was never meant to be a giant jungle gym.

Of more concern to Jade was the noise that she could no longer hear. The ghostly humming had stopped.

A few more rungs, and Jade's feet touched solid ground. She found herself in the gap between the wall of dirt and the steel skeleton. She didn't have time to think about how creepy and cramped it was. She didn't have time to be scared. A wedge of runny concrete was rumbling toward her like a mud slide.

She knelt down. There was a tarpaulin over the lowest layer of horizontal rods. Underneath it, she could just make out Luke's hands and feet fastened with plastic straps to the bars. Luke himself was covered with a thick blanket. Half of it was plastered with wet concrete.

"Hang on," she shouted.

She yanked the tarpaulin out of the way to get the light that she needed. Then she leaned into the cage and grimaced at the red stains around Luke's wrists. He'd been struggling. And losing a lot of blood. She snipped the plastic straps as quickly as her fumbling fingers allowed and dropped the wire cutters.

Grasping his arms, she tugged with all of her remaining strength, dragging the lump that was Luke toward the side of the hole. The blanket stayed where it was. For a few seconds, it formed a perfect mold of half of his body. Then the soft concrete crushed the shape, crawled over the blanket, and toward them both. Having been denied its victim, it seemed to want to reclaim him.

At Jade's feet was a mangled version of her boyfriend. She thought that he was unconscious, but his eyes flickered open weakly. She picked at the edge of the tape on his cheek and then ripped it away from his mouth. In a rasping voice that she barely recognized, he said, "Heard you arguing with Malc."

Jade almost laughed. Almost cried. "He deserved it. Stupid machine."

But Luke had sunk into oblivion again.

The spreading concrete lapped around her shoes like an incoming tide, trying to encircle and swallow Luke once more. They were trapped in the corner.

Jade looked up. There was no way that she could carry him to safety. He was too big, and she was exhausted. Besides, there was only enough space for one person at a time to squeeze through the gap. Completely stumped, she was powerless to stop the tears rolling down her cheeks. She'd gotten this far—she'd found Luke—but she was about to fail. She couldn't rescue him. She could barely save herself. If it meant leaving Luke, she didn't want to save herself.

She bent down, grabbed his limp arm, and shook him. "Wake up. Come on, Luke! You've got to wake up!"

But there was no reaction. He didn't even seem to be breathing. He was utterly lifeless.

"Hey, there!" a builder called down to her. "Grab this. It's a hoist. Wrap the end bit around him. We'll do the rest."

Jade knew that there was no such thing as the supernatural, but right now, exhausted and afraid, that voice sounded as if it had come from a guardian angel.

Chapter Thirty

The emergency medical team that Malc had summoned resuscitated Luke as soon as the crane lifted him out of the pit. Then the paramedics stopped his bleeding, but they were more concerned about the effects of a dose of tranquilizer that would have stopped a hippopotamus in its tracks. They gave him oxygen and yohimbine. They talked urgently between themselves about organ failure and overwhelming inflammation. They agreed that a local general hospital could not do the job and called for a helicopter to take him to a specialist poisoning unit at York Hospital. They also picked their most experienced member to travel with Luke to keep him alive during the airlift.

With her hand over her mouth, Jade stood behind the paramedics and watched them deal with the crisis. Luke was a terrible color. His brown skin had paled. In patches, it was as gray as the concrete that had almost engulfed him. The staining on his cheeks told her that he'd vomited on the way up. Now, he was utterly unresponsive. He was bloated, and he looked like an old man. Jade felt useless. Sidelined.

When the medical team strapped Luke to a board, picked him up, and headed for the heliport, she followed them. "I'm going with him," she told them.

"There'll be a paramedic and his mobile on board. That's it."

"No," she replied. "There'll be me as well."

"It is well known," Malc said, "that comatose patients often respond better to the voices of people that they love than they do to drugs, medical procedures, and doctors. For that reason, Jade Vernon should accompany the patient."

Surprised, the chief paramedic stared at Malc. "You don't have the power to make that decision."

At once, Jade recognized the female voice that came out of Malc. "Yes, it does. It has the absolute confidence of The Authorities. Jade Vernon will remain with our investigator at all times."

Jade watched Luke remove the headphones from his ears. He still had the impressive battle scar on his cheek and another on his neck, but he was the right color and his eyes were bright again. "What do you think, then?" she asked. "It's only another minute or so, but I'm going to throw in drums, bass, and strings next. It'll take me a bit longer."

Head resting on a mass of pillows, Luke beamed at her. "Stunning. And fantastic for humming."

"Well, that wasn't exactly my top priority, but the way things turned out, it's a good thing. Anyway, when are they going to let you out of here?"

Luke shrugged. "Malc's set up a supply of

pomegranates. They're what has wiped out the last of the tranquilizer. The rest of the food's really good. You visit and bring me your latest pieces. The Authorities haven't given me my next job yet, and everyone's dashing around taking care of me. Why should I want to leave?"

"Because you're getting soft, that's why. And I might not be able to visit anymore."

Alarmed, Luke asked, "Why not?"

"I might be in prison. Malc reported me for impersonating a forensic investigator."

Luke could tell from her tone that she wasn't taking the accusation seriously. With a wry smile and a sigh of relief, he nodded. "Yeah. That sounds like Malc."

Jade shook her head. "I don't know how you cope with him."

"When the hospital realizes that I'm not sick—just lying here having a vacation—I might be put on your case. I might have to investigate you."

"I was lying about prison. I've been let off. The Authorities sent me a message saying that they wouldn't be pursuing the charge against me. Nice of them, isn't it?"

A girl walked—almost skipped—through Luke's open door. She was around ten years old. She had a small bag slung over one shoulder, and she gripped a tall and shiny pyramid in both hands.

"Hey! Look at you," Luke said to her. "A lot better than when I first saw you. Are you going back to school?"

Beaming, she nodded. "I'm better."

"You beat me," Luke said with a smile. "I thought I'd be out before you."

Nyree looked down at the heavy ornament she was carrying. Its sides were very smooth, bright, and a lush shade of green. "If I gave you this, you'd get well, but . . ." She hugged it to her chest. "I can't."

Luke smiled at her. "It's okay. I'm almost better again anyway." Humoring her, he added, "You keep it. If it's a lucky charm, it'll make sure you never have to come back."

"It's made out of jade," Nyree told him, "and jade's good for you."

Luke exchanged a smile with Jade and then looked back at Nyree. "That's true. I'll let you in on a secret." Almost whispering, he said, "I've got Jade as well. Saved my life."

From the doorway, an instructor called, "Come on, Nyree. That's enough. Say your good-byes to the nurses, and we can go."

As soon as the little girl left, Jade pulled a face, thumped Luke's arm, and muttered, "Cringe. You *are* getting soft!"

Making them both jump, another visitor flew into the room.

"I have undergone a complete overhaul," Malc announced. "All my systems are operating at optimum."

"Oh, great," Jade muttered.

"Glad to hear it," said Luke.

Malc wasted no time. "A search of the veterinary surgeon's quarters revealed two pairs of sky-blue socks and a container of powder for treating athlete's foot. His shoe size was ten inches. Ian Pritchard has been charged with murder, malicious wounding, attempted murder of a forensic investigator and a rifle shooter, electromagnetic interference with a computer network, and seven counts of property damage. One of these caused the deaths of seventy-six people on Flight GGW17, and another resulted in the deaths of two workers in the main stadium."

"Hang on," Jade said. "Aren't you going to ask Luke if he's feeling better?"

"Unnecessary. I have access to FI Harding's medical file. The patient has recovered sufficiently to be discharged within twenty-four hours."

Luke grinned and shook his head. "Well, it's nice to see *you* back on your feet, Malc."

"I do not possess . . ."

The remainder of Malc's response was lost in their laughter.

TRACES: BLOOD BROTHER

Nyree was nervous and scared, but she was also spellbound. With her personal tutor, she'd come to a halt beside a rock garden of colorful heathers that surrounded a scruffy wooden hut in the picturesque riverside area of York. "Well," she said with a tremor in her voice, "this must be it." Nyree's sunken eyes were fixed on the shack that had once been very fancy. Its bright paint was now faded and peeling, revealing rotten wood underneath. Even though the cabin had seen better days, its windows still had displays of cheerful, homemade trinkets. They were the reason that Nyree Max had sought out the trailer before going back into the hospital.

When Mr. Peacock opened the door cautiously, a distinct smell of herbs and spices wafted over Nyree. Scented candles filled the place, and an old man was sitting behind a counter, tying together sprigs of a deep green and crimson heather. Nyree took one look at him and knew immediately that he was the artist with the peculiar reputation. She climbed the two steps and entered uneasily. At least in the shack, the blinding winter sunshine would no longer burn her eyes and blur her vision.

The old man raised his face toward his visitors. He cast a dismissive glance at Mr. Peacock, but he gazed intently at Nyree. His expression suggested a mixture of kindness and pity. He did not utter a word.

The door closed behind Mr. Peacock, shutting Nyree and her tutor inside. The flimsy cabin was curiously quiet, cut off from the rest of York. Around three of its walls were shelves, and in the middle was a long table. All of the available surfaces were covered with the artist's goods: cute cats and dogs delicately carved out of wood, countless model dancers in pink or blue with silver headdresses, dainty porcelain figurines, candles infused with herbs, ceramic boxes, and much more. Carefully, Nyree picked up a few of the mementoes, one after another, but felt no attachment to them. She replaced them quickly.

Making her way down the aisle between the table and the right-hand shelves, Nyree hesitated by a selection of jade figurines and jewelry. Handwritten on a little card among the trinkets were the words "Items in hard jade bring the owner good health." Reading the label, Nyree allowed herself a sad smile. Hoping that it was true, she picked up a jade squirrel, weighed it in her hand, and then put it back in the display. There were a lot of incredible carvings in jade: coiled snakes, pigs, grotesque people, all kinds of things. None of them grabbed her attention.

A deep green pyramid caught Nyree's eye. It was solid,

smooth, and simple. No fancy carving, just three plain, slick surfaces in dark green. She put out her trembling hand toward it but did not clasp the ornament. For a moment, she felt frightened of it. She told herself not to be silly. She tried to convince herself that her unease had nothing to do with the pyramid. She was just afraid of letting the beautiful charm slip from her fingers and crash to the floor. She was weak, of course, but not that weak. Her eyesight was wobbly but not that wobbly. The tingling in her spine and the thudding inside her head were her illness. Those feelings didn't stop her from holding an ornament. She reached out for it.

The old man behind the counter picked up some more heather, but he didn't do anything with it. Instead, he watched the ten-year-old girl closely as she took the pyramid in her right hand and placed it on her left palm. A strange smile came to his lined face when he saw her shiver.

Around eight inches tall, the three green sides of the pyramid were astonishingly shiny and reminded Nyree of mirrors. Some of the images reflected there seemed close, some far away, but none real. The bottom of the pyramid was black and totally unlike a mirror. Light seemed to disappear into the matt surface rather than bounce off it. She had to fight the urge to drop the sculpture when the icy base contacted the skin of her palm.

"What have you found?" Mr. Peacock asked her in a voice that sounded too loud. "Not the most decorative, is it?"

"No, but . . ." Nyree muttered without looking up from her hypnotic find.

"But, what?"

Nyree had been feeling sick and unsteady, but the jade pyramid had distracted her. "This is what I want."

"Really? Are you sure? There are a lot of nicer . . ."

"I'm sure."

Mr. Peacock shrugged. "Take it up to the man, then."

When Nyree walked toward him, the old man stood up and nodded knowingly. "That's very special, darling. Most singular." His voice was slow, as if he was not used to the language. He stared into Nyree's face. "I can see why it's chosen you."

Nyree winced as Mr. Peacock corrected his faltering grammar. "You mean, why Nyree's chosen it."

"Do I?" the artist retorted without even glancing at Mr. Peacock. "Look." He came out from behind the counter and took Nyree's arm. Realizing that Nyree's hearing was weak, he spoke louder. "This is what you do, darling. Listen. You touch one of the green sides against here." His wrinkled hand went to Nyree's forehead. "Then you put it by your bed, you see, and sleep with a lamp on so the pyramid's shadow falls on you through the night."

Amused, Mr. Peacock asked, "And what does that do?"

"*That*," he answered impatiently, as if a tutor should have known, "heals the sick."

"How quaint."

"Quaint?" the artist replied, clearly confused and possibly insulted.

Mr. Peacock backtracked. "It's . . . um . . . a charming tradition."

The man scowled at him and then turned toward Nyree again. "No one touches or disturbs you during pyramid time. You see? Afterward, you return the pyramid to me. It does not work again. It's like a toy with batteries. Understand? It runs down after a cure. It's yours to use and then it's mine to recharge."

Mr. Peacock produced his identity card. "Are you saying that we're going to borrow it and not own it?"

The man shook his head and waved away the plastic card. Talking solely to Nyree again, he said, "It's yours, darling. You use it well. But only once and never again. Twice is very dangerous." He wagged a knobbly finger at her and frowned. "Bring it back to me."

"All right," Nyree said quietly, hugging the precious trinket.

"Good," he replied. "You know, I'm glad you came to my trailer."

Nyree didn't know what to reply, so she said, "Thank you."

With a wistful expression on his withered face, the old man watched his visitors leave. Then he walked to the window and gazed at Nyree through the filmy glass until she was out of sight.

Back on the walkway, out in the brightness of the real world, Mr. Peacock mumbled, "Weird! Different culture altogether. Still, no harm done."

The low sunlight stung Nyree's eyes and brought immediate tears. The hammering in her skull started once again. But despite this, she smiled to herself.

For the first time in ages, Nyree felt great. Her head was free of the crippling migraines. She didn't feel sore, sick, and wobbly. Her vision wasn't flickering and blurred. She walked—almost skipped—out of her own room and in through the forensic investigator's open door. Nyree liked Luke Harding. He was tall and nice and sick like her. Or, rather, like she used to be. She had her bag over one shoulder and she gripped her shiny pyramid in both hands to make sure that she didn't drop it.

"Hey! Look at you," Luke said. "A lot better than when I first saw you. Are you going back to school?"

She nodded, unable to keep a big grin from her face. "I'm better."

"You beat me," Luke replied. "I thought I'd be out before you."

Nyree looked down at her heavy pyramid. "If I gave you this, you'd get well, but . . ." She hugged it to her chest. "I can't."

"It's okay. I'm almost better again anyway." Smiling at her, Luke said, "You keep it. If it's a lucky charm, it'll make sure you never have to come back."

"It's made out of jade," said Nyree. Thinking of the label on the shelf in that peculiar trailer, she added, "And jade's good for you."

Nyree watched as Luke glanced at his other visitor. Maybe she was his girlfriend. Even so, Nyree didn't know why they exchanged a secret smile.

Luke lowered his voice. "That's true. I'll let you in on a secret. I've got Jade as well. Saved my life."

Nyree was trying to figure out what he meant when Mr. Peacock, lurking at the door, called, "Come on, Nyree. That's enough. Say your good-byes to the nurses, and we can go."

It was the first of March, and the annual celebration for the coming to power of The Authorities was in full swing. Robotic clowns with ridiculously long legs and large feet padded along York's riverside walkway, making a variety of robotic laughing noises. The air was rich with the sulfurous smell of gunpowder and the strong aroma of spices from the barbecue stalls by the bridge. The flashing lights or the colorful fairground rides were reflected in the Ouse river. Firecrackers jumped around, making the sound of gunfire. Every few seconds, a rocket shot into the sky, exploded with the deafening noise of a cannon, and formed a huge, vivid mushroom of stars, illuminating the city. At once, the bloom of light began to weep. Sparkling tears of blue and red and yellow and white fell like rain.

Nyree Max stood empty-handed on the riverbank. Straining her neck for a while, she watched the big wheel as it rotated slowly, taking sightseers 200 feet up in glass pods. From the top, they'd have fabulous views of the vibrant city bathed in spectacular light. Nyree wasn't going on the wheel because she got jittery with height. Besides, she was fascinated more by the Ouse river itself. It had come alive with hundreds of tiny flames. Huge numbers of candles floated gently downstream on small beautiful boats made from leaves. The old man in the riverside shack had probably made quite a few of them.

Most people who pushed out their waterborne candles did it for fun—because it had become a tradition. They wanted to see their own mini boat jostling with all the others, making a stunning display like an unhurried procession of fireflies. A few superstitious people believed that, when they released their candle into the flow, all of their bad luck and bad health would also drift away. Nyree's own candle joined the rest and glided down the river, along with her disabling migraines.

Nyree didn't know if she believed in the supernatural, but the pyramid that she'd just taken back to the trailer had worked, so maybe that made her a believer. Unsure, though, she let the question go like a balloon released by a tired child.

By the frequent flashes of light outside his windows, Crawford Gallagher examined the pyramid that the girl had returned. As always when he had to recharge it, he felt queasy. Turning the used pyramid in his shrunken hands, he gazed at the three faces of hard jade. They were an indefinable deep green speckled with the reflections of bright bursts of fireworks. The multicolored stars glittered in the mirrorlike surfaces, but the bottom of the pyramid was different. When Crawford looked at it, he shuddered unpleasantly. No reflections, no light, no life. After a cure, it always appeared to be a hole. He imagined that he could put his hand right into it and feel . . . nothing. He couldn't touch the inside of the pyramid any more than he could reach out on a dark night and touch the infinite sky. Of course, the base wasn't a hole or a tunnel or infinity. It was just a dull surface, used to regenerate the pyramid's healing power.

Carefully, Crawford took the vial of deep red fluid on his counter and unscrewed the top. Then he tilted the container over the bottom of the pyramid. The fresh human blood ran out sluggishly and dropped onto that cold surface, giving the jade pyramid fresh life.